# come
# hear
## the
# Whisper
## of
# time

## BARBARA
## J. DUELL

Come Hear the Whisper of Time

Published by Shadow Wind, LLC, Fountain Hills, AZ 85268
Printed in the United States of America

ISBN 978-0-9911192-3-3 (trade paperback)
ISBN 978-0-9911192-2-6 (e-book)

Cover and formatting: Streetlight Graphics

*may you find*
*peace in Living,*
*Loving and Remembering*

*Barbara J Shell*

# Dedication

This book is dedicated to my family and
To anyone who has ever loved and lost

# Table of Contents

# Acknowledgement

**M**Y LIFE IS THE SUM of my faith and the love of my family. As I have journeyed through the years, I pray I have been worthy. I reach out to you now from within my soul, hoping to find a refuge, a safe place to share what has gathered within me from the beginning.

# Introduction

## The Road Map

THERE WAS A TIME, REALLY not that long ago, when I walked a tight rope without a net. I bordered on the edge of madness, although to an observer I might have appeared stable. But I barely functioned, lost in a fog that held me aloft, yet not far enough away from the anguish that sought to pull me into darkness, and I was afraid.

Lady Tragedy had arrived on our doorstep and looked like she was prepared to stay for a long time, or so it seemed.

If we think about this journey we call life, we know that it does not go on forever and that we will have to draw on an inner strength when it ends for those we love. But no matter how realistic our thinking, the pain and anguish that accompanies this knowledge is almost impossible to accept.

During our life time, we will be asked to walk down the road accompanied by grief, and of course, we would rather not. Grief is a terrible companion, one that is hard to define because each one of us will experience this emotion differently. Some will hide in denial; others will play games, and there are those who will even lose their grip on reality.

Recovery, ending this relationship with grief and anguish, is more than a multi-tiered process. I know, for I have walked hand in hand with all these emotions—two steps forward and ten back. I put on blinders as I tittered close to the edge during the day, trying to hold on tight until I could escape into the privacy of night to search for answers, trying to find the door out and away from this terrible place I never ever want to be, but I would just end up sitting in the dark and hiding from life.

As my broken heart tried to mend after the loss of my sons, I reached deep within my soul, even as I sought to run from the pain. So many friends offered to help. They meant well... There were so many wonderful and caring people who only wanted to see me smile again. I read books. The library is full of advice, some written by professionals and others by people just like me. But nothing really helped. I even signed up for a course relating to managing grief. I think this class helped more than anything I had tried so far, but not as you might think. I sat around a table with ten other people, and as I listened to their stories, I wanted to get up and run out the door. Many of these people had been attending this class for years. One man was terribly upset because he thought his children were not properly grieving the loss of their mother. When he first started to speak, I just assumed her passing was a recent event, but she had been gone for over ten years. Please understand that I felt so sad for this man and his family, and I do not minimize his anguish. That's one of the wretched things about suffering. It attacks us all differently, but that experience opened my eyes to the fact that I could continue to grieve, to muck around in my self-pity and hide from life, or I could get myself in hand and go searching for the old me, the one who, if I were honest with myself, already knew where to find the road back into the sunlight.

I realized if I continued to rant silently, to tear at my heart and soul, I would be wasting what had only been loaned to me for a while—my life. How could I honor those I love so much if I continued to waste what they had given up? And so began the continuation of what had been ordained for me long ago in my book of days. It was not easy; it never is, but you do it. You just do.

Everyone reaches for a different lifeline, and after finding myself again, I turned to writing. And all that I have written here, except what I share about sailing, my mom and dad, and my sons and saying good-bye, is fiction.

There is no rhyme or reason, no theme for the words that have found their way into this book, except maybe the feeling we experience when we love and are loved. I had no idea what I was doing, only that when I wrote, I journeyed to another place, a space not crowded with sadness. I wrote short stories. I tried to write funny stuff but ripped that up and started over, always returning to the indescribably wonderful feeling love conveys.

So I have written about love: new beginnings, relationships that need care... my love of the sea. There are stories that will ask you to open your mind and just imagine as you travel to another dimension, a premise requiring faith and trust.

Of course, it was not hard to recount a part of what I loved and admired about my mom and dad. Add to that the memories of my sons coming of age and this small book, *Come Hear the Whisper of Time,* was born. It is a collection of fact, fiction, and fantasy, a journey to another place

*bjd*

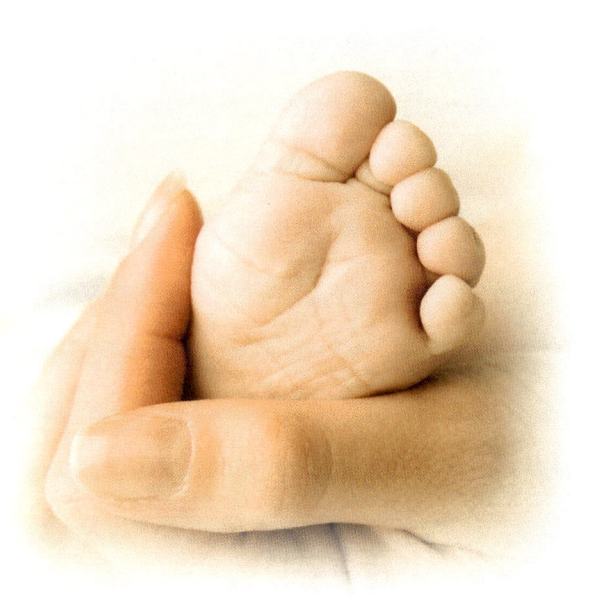

# *Beginnings*

*I feel so humble each time I touch my child, overwhelmed
by the realization that this miracle of life, this gift from
God, is truly part of me, of my spirit and my soul.*

# *Reflections*

S TREAKS OF SUNLIGHT FILTER THROUGH the grilled window, warming my face as I carefully ease out of bed. I don't want to wake him; we've had such a restless night, and he needs his sleep. I turn to look at him and quiver, a feeling as elusive as the silvery fingers of the early morning sun that fills our loft. I still cannot believe he is here nor think of what I have even done to deserve this gift.

I reach for my robe and descend the old wooden staircase. I've forgotten my slippers and the cold stone floor tickles my feet as I move quietly toward the kitchen. As the aroma of brewing coffee fills the air, I listen for sounds from the open room above and smile. David is so clever. The man I love has taken an old rundown cottage and made it our home. And although he couldn't find a way to give me a real castle, he's built us a magical kingdom that seems to reach beyond the Milky Way and straight past tomorrow.

But I can't stay away. With a mug of steamy coffee in my hand, I retrace my steps and stop at the foot of the bed and watch this person I love with every fiber of what I am or hope to be. An involuntary shiver charges through me, a thrill so strong I shake and spill hot coffee from the mug.

What will I do when he leaves me? And he will. Can I let

him go with a smile? Without angry words, without a tear on my face, a tear that might cause him pain even though he will be the one leaving? What will I do when he needs more than I can give? My heart races, pounds in my chest. It's so strong I fear he can hear it.

But why am I doing this... standing here fighting my fears? I've just found him. I take a deep breath and tell myself not to dwell on his leaving; I must cherish every minute of time we have now.

He stirs, pulls his knees to his chest, and I hear his soft sleep sounds, sounds lost in the bedcovers, their meaning locked in his dreams. He is so handsome, such dark hair, so full. His eyes are a color beyond description, a gray that can turn to deep violet with the changing of the light or his mood. As I sip the cooled coffee, part of me wants to wake him, to wrap my arms around him and hold him tightly against my aching chest.

As if hearing my wish, he rolls over and stretches, easing slowly from his slumber. He opens his eyes, searching, and then smiles when he sees me standing there, watching him, and loving him. I place the mug on the side table, drop my robe, and crawl back into bed. Even as he reaches for me, I gather him into my arms just as I longed to do a moment ago. He nudges into my gown, seeking my breast, and I draw in the smell of him as my lips gently touch the top of his head.

I open my gown, and he finds what he seeks, and as my tiny son seeks nourishment, as he takes me into his mouth, I close my eyes and my sad thoughts of moments ago slip away, set free to chase after the bright sunlight. For I know my child will need me for a long time to come, and when it is time for him to leave, to find his way in the world, I won't cry. I won't let him see my tears even though they will be tears of pride, of thankfulness for having had him near me for so long, tears of love that bind us together, a bond as strong and clear as the path that leads beyond the Milky Way and straight past tomorrow.

# Leaving The Nest

THE AIR IS BRISK, CLEANSED by the rain. I breathe deeply and relish the stillness of dawn. This is my favorite time, a special time when I can silently witness the birth of a new day as the first rays of the sun erase the lingering shadows from my garden.

My eyes and ears focus on the tiny nest hidden under the eaves of the patio. She is up early to feed her babies, but why am I surprised? For weeks now I have watched the small fly-fisher rushing about, searching for the perfect spot to build her nest. Nothing was too good for her new home, and like a seasoned contractor, she worked for days building a safe place to deposit her eggs, carrying twigs and moss, bits of carpet threads found here and there.

Then came the sitting—the waiting—and as she hastened their growth with her body, carefully turning each globe, did she ever wonder if she would be able to feed them, to keep them from harm? This time of waiting was short for her, only a few weeks. I had nine months to ponder such thoughts and to conquer my fears.

As she flies back and forth catering nourishment to her young, I marvel at her dedication, her almost frantic drive to fulfill their needs, never stopping to rest, never thinking of her own needs. Her scurries to and fro remind me of another time, a time when I too hurried about: the

21

regular trips to preschool, to Scouts and Little League, the cuts and bruises, fighting over the car and staying out too late, the scraping together enough money for university.

My house is quiet now. So different from years ago, when we used this early hour to search for missing football shoes or the panic to finish a report due by first period. We'd pile into the car and race off on our way, circle back for a forgotten lunch box, and as I delivered each one of my prized cargo to their assigned destination, I'd map out the rest of the day, mentally plotting all variables, times, and locations, who needed to be where and when. And somewhere between doing the laundry and grocery shopping, I'd ponder my logic, or the lack of, my reason for wanting so many children and that's when I would smile.

Because I was the lucky one, the one with the valuable and exciting ticket for the best trip on Earth, the ticket that allowed me passage as a major participant on their wondrous adventure toward manhood.

The fly-fisher pulls me back to the present as her high shrill resonates across the patio. Flight school is in session, and I cannot help but smile as I watch the two little birds racing under the eaves, flapping their wings as they try to imitate their mom before returning safely to the nest.

When her babies grow and leave home, will they ever seek her out again? Will she feel sad when they fly away, or a sense of pride knowing that, in such a short time, she has taught them enough to survive in Mother Nature's scheme of things?

My son called last night, and his words echo through my mind. He just wanted to talk, nothing special he said laughingly. He just wanted to hear my voice. Does he know the joy this brings me?

As I watch the rising sun, I wonder if I taught my sons enough. Did I teach them to love, to be honest with others but especially with themselves? Was I selfish? Did I keep them dependent on me, or did I cut the strings and let them go, helping them to believe they really could go out into the world and survive?

The wind is up, but I feel warm as memories caress my heart, and as I watch the small fly-fisher divide her food between two gaping beaks, I remind myself that I did the best I could. I gave them all my love... all the discipline and knowledge I possessed. Was it enough? I hope so, but only the future knows for sure.

# *Forgiving*

**D**ARKNESS WRAPPED THE EMPTY HOUSE like an elusive shroud. The scent of night-blooming jasmine filled the air, gently tossed here and there by an invading breeze from the open patio door. Even before his eyes adjusted to the dark, he knew she was not in the house.

He bent to pick up her book on the floor by the phone. By the open door, he found her shoes, on the patio, her sweater. Just like crumbs of sadness dropped to mark the way, he gathered each piece of her until he stood at the bottom of a large tree.

How could he explain to her how sorry he was for today? Sure his life was complicated; work was tough, and money was tight, but that was no excuse. She was the best of all he was, and life without her was simply unimaginable. He should not have lost his temper. She didn't deserve this, especially now with the baby due so soon.

He gazed in amazement, wondering how she had managed to climb up the ladder and into the tree house in her condition, but it really didn't matter. What mattered now was making her believe how much he loved her. Slowly he climbed the wooden ladder as he called out her name.

She sat huddled in a corner with her knees pulled as close to her chest as the baby would allow. The light from a tiny candle formed a halo around her bent head, like a far-off star, brilliant though small.

He knew she knew he was there, but he also knew she would not look up nor offer to talk about what had driven her to this special place. He crossed the few steps and dropped down beside her. His fingers lightly brushed across her tear-stained cheek, lifting a dark curl off her neck, and then he kissed the spot where it had rested. He felt her instantly tremble, but she didn't pull away. He almost wished she had as tears broke free from her swollen eyes and streamed down her face.

He took her into his arms and held her close to his chest as his heart pounded against hers. "Please don't cry. I am so sorry. I'm such a thoughtless jerk. I didn't mean to yell at you over the phone. It's just that well... No, I won't make an excuse. There is none for what I did. Please don't cry; please don't be mad at me."

He took her face between his hands and brushed away her tears with his thumbs. He kissed her wet eyes, the tip of her nose, and her quivering lips, telling her how much he loved her.

"Can you forgive me? Please say you're not mad at me. I couldn't stand that, not now, not ever."

"It's because I'm so fat. I know it is. I'm not pretty anymore. How could you possibly love me when I look like this? I can't even tie my shoes." She all but whispered her words, but their meaning stripped the beat from his heart.

*My God! She thinks it's her fault that I yelled at her.* "Oh, baby, no. It's not your fault. My love, you are beautiful and wonderful. Please don't cry. Here, dry your eyes. Look at me. I love you so much. More than I ever thought I could love anyone. And you did nothing wrong, except to love such an inconsiderate fool, a fool who doesn't have enough sense to know how lucky he is. And you are not fat. You're carrying our baby. You know you really should not have climbed up here. You could have hurt yourself. There now, that's better."

Only the sound of her lingering sobs pushed at the quiet that filled the tiny space lodged high in the old tree. And as its delicate leaves danced in the breeze, the moon and the stars watched in wonder as he kissed her with all the love heaven allowed. His hands caressed the body they knew so well as his kiss deepened, drawing them closer than any words. They shed their clothes and loved each other like fleeting moths, lingering at each stage of passion only long enough to relish the song, the music heard only by those who are filled with the rhyme of giving.

And in that tiny sanctuary—as the white moon blazed in a blanket of stars and the summer breeze carried all the anger and hurt and misunderstanding to another place—an unborn child smiled.

# *Joy*

*There are times when my heart flutters—*
*I feel so alive and delighted by the sheer joy*
*of being loved—of loving.*

1. Out of the Mist
2. The White Raven
3. The Song of the Wren

# Out Of The Mist

T HE HEAVENS CRIED LAST NIGHT—A torrent of tears, sent with a force so powerful the earth shook. But with the tears came cleansing, a rebirth that left the world around us fresh and with hope.

I awake, still laden with sorrow but also with the need to see what truths have survived. Carefully I spread my cloak upon the damp ground and open my bag of emotions. One by one I place each feeling on the scarlet cloth. First I touch Joy, then Confusion, followed by several Misunderstandings. I rest, for a while—trembling—then draw a deep breath before I continue.

My hand reaches slowly within the velvety folds and I feel the heat and know, even before I withdraw my hand, that I hold Love. Or should I call it Need or Lust, maybe only Desire? But it doesn't matter, because called by any name, the fire is just as hot—burns with such fury it can cause pleasure beyond belief—or intense pain.

But I do withdraw my hand and gaze at the heat of Love. I try to place it next to the others, but it will not let go. It wraps around my fingers, seeps into my skin, and travels throughout my body, seeking to make me its prisoner. I have no will of my own and I know I will soon be lost. But then Reason moves on its own from the mouth of the velvet bag and meets Love head on.

I turn to run away. This is not a battle I want nor one I can control; the outcome is simply not mine to decide, but I cannot run. I can only stand and watch and hope and pray and muffle my doubts because even if I were able to choose, I could not.

Does Reason face Love or only an Imposter? And if this is an Imposter, will it last? Or will it fade away, diminished by the brilliance of the shimmering galaxies? Slowly from the folds of velvet comes Logic holding the hand of Remembrance, coaxing her out and into the sunlight, and she's wrapped in a mantle of Truth.

I marvel as Logic and Remembrance mate and merge into one, and the metamorphosis stills the air as I wait, not daring to move. I watch as Beauty and the power of Creation give birth to Innocence who rises before me.

I am touched by the hand of Innocence who gently lifts away the sheer veil of Confusion that covers my eyes so I might see Truth as never before. She strips away the silken fabric that distorts the veracity of the past, and I am bathed in the Glory of Reminiscence

Overpowered by this knowledge, I raise my arms to the heavens and bask in the Radiance of a Thousand Candles. For I know now this is Love, and I see his face, he who gives reason to the center of my life, who has never been far, just waiting for me at the opposite end of Eternity, only waiting for me to call out his name.

# The White Raven

SLOWLY SHE SOARS ACROSS THE palette of the Sky, gathering a kaleidoscope of color on the tip of her wings. Twirling, stretching her snow-like plumage until shadows darken the ground below, she climbs to the Moon to bid him goodnight as the last Stars watch her dance and the Sun begins to rise and share her joy.

Today is the seventh day of the seventh year and emotions sent far beyond this time mix in her wake. The Winds gather from the East, lifting her again to soar above Earth, but flight becomes secondary as she recalls the last time they were together. This image floats before her keen eyes—vivid, like the Moon reflecting off the stillness of the Sea—of his handsome face and the fire of his touch, of his love. Yes, she waits and remembers.

There was a time in the beginning when the People did not follow the Laws of the Great Spirit and they were sent away to a place without warmth. Only those who lived beyond the Arch of the Sky knew the comfort of fire, and the keeper of this fire was called Lightning.

Each year the wise men among the People would go to her. They would tell Lightning of their sorrow, how they had changed and now lived by the old ways, but she would not listen. They pleaded their case to her mate, Thunder, begging him to intervene for them and convince Lightning that they had learned their lesson well and they needed the fire.

They could not convince her, not at first, but after a time, Lightning set forth a challenge. She would place the sacred fire in the middle of an island, in the hollow of the Sycamore tree. If there lived among the People one with the strength and courage to cross the water and carry the fire back to their village, they could keep the flame forever.

The People were overjoyed. This would be easy, no challenge at all, not with so many brave young warriors living within their village. They would cross the water and return with the flame, but as time flew away, not one of the warriors brought back the treasure. Many drowned in the Sea. Others faltered, their hands burned when they tried to lift the fire from the Sycamore. Soon the tales of failure rose higher than the courage of the young warriors and none would take up the task.

It was at this time that all living things spoke the same language and they shared all knowledge within the village. The gloom of failure touched them all except one, one who refused to accept defeat. There lived among the People a pair of White Ravens. Their love and devotion to each other set an example to all who would mate for life. One night at the tribal meeting, the great White Raven, with his mate by his side, spoke to the council. He told the Elders he would go to the island and bring back the fire so the People would know the warmth of the flame. His strength and wisdom were legendary, like the ancient People from the beginning of time.

Early the next morning he embraced his mate. Even without words, his message was clear. His eyes softened, full of love for his white beauty as he reassured her no harm would befall him and he would return with the fire.

She watched with the others as he shot into the heavens and out of sight. For hours she waited by the edge of the Sea, searching the horizon for his giant wings to appear in the Sky. She waited until the Sun rose and set, then rose again, and still he did not return. Refusing food and water, she waited by the Sea. Her love would return, she told herself repeatedly, and he would find her waiting; she would be the first thing he saw when he crossed the cobalt Sky, bearing the flame.

But no matter how hard she vowed not to close her eyes, sleep finally claimed its toll. Raven rested on the shore until a pounding in her heart stirred her soul. Rising, she searched again across the Sea and near the top of Sky's Arch, and then she saw a faint light. Closer it came, and she knew it must be her beloved carrying the precious flame. She called the People to the shore as she continued to watch the glow in the darkness, each second drawing it closer to the village. The People cheered at the welcome sight, but it was not the light she sought, only the first glimpse of his giant white wings... wings that would soon hold her in an embrace, an embrace warmer and more life giving than all the fire in the universe.

He circled the village and dropped the bolt of fire into the sacred caldron that had known the flame in another time. He rose high above the village, above the People who watched in confusion at the sight of him, who dropped to the ground and turned their eyes away from that which he had become, fearing he had not only brought the fire, but an evil curse to their village.

The great White Raven was now as black as the hour of midnight, darker than Sky without the Moon and Stars, and they were afraid.

"Come to me," the Black Raven called to his mate. "If you are not afraid, fly high to the open temple where the un-bodied keepers of Knowledge and Wisdom dwell and I will meet you there. But come only if you can still look upon me with love alive in your eyes." Then he was gone, dissolving into the night.

Even before his words drifted away on the chilling

breeze, she took to the air, and using all the strength her small heart could gather, she flew to their secret place and found him waiting for her. Raven knew, even though his plumage looked darker than death, he was still her true and only mate, and she soared to him with all the trust and love allowed by the Spirits to one heart.

"You must listen to my words, for we have little time. I tried so hard to do what I had promised, but the true meaning of the challenge was not honorable, only a jest. Lightning never meant for us to have the flame. She toyed with me, at first mocking me, telling me I had not the will to do what she would require, and all the time, Thunder laughed in the background. I ignored her taunting and reached for the fire, but she caused the flame to rise and scorched my body."

The giant black bird pulled his mate closer to his body as he continued. "I tried to explain that I was only the courier and that the fire was not for me, but for the children, to warm them, to cook their food. I told her we needed the fire to light the lodge on dark nights so the history of our People could be told to the young ones so they could know of their heritage. It was no use; my words were flung into the air just as ash from the bed of the flame rose into the heavens, blown about by the roar of Thunder's laughter."

White Raven sought words to comfort her mate, soothing words to turn his mind away from the terrifying images he relived and to loosen the tightening in her chest as he told of the cruel way Lightning and Thunder had dishonored his plight.

"At last she offered a trade. You must listen very carefully, my heart, for to gain the fire I had to forfeit our lives... the life and happiness we have always known. I had no choice. This was the only way the People would ever possess the flame. This night will be our last one for many years. We will not meet again until the seventh day of the seventh year after this Moon. Do not cry, my love, for this night we have the power to share our love as humans, shape-shifting into a man and a woman. And each time we meet, every seven years, we will meet and love this way."

And so it was that this night of deep sorrow became a revelation of joy as the keepers of Knowledge and Wisdom made them a bed of softened grass and then stood guard as they reached out to each other. The man watched with pride, with desire and need—emotions known to all, not just mortal man—as she transformed before his eyes into a woman as beautiful as all creation. She lowered her gown of simple cloth, a stark contrast to the unearthly beauty of the emerald trees and turf surrounding them. He stood very still as she began to unbind her long white hair that shimmered like sunlight even in the darkness of the night.

They came together with a gentle touch, sent like a symphony to fill the hollow chambers of their souls, and Love was the Master of the Song. Later, as they pretended dawn would never come, they breathed deeply of the aroma of Life, of each other, memorizing each movement, each special quality to sustain them for all the tomorrows of the next seven years. Tears welled in her eyes, but she did not cry, just whispered to the Spirits, to the yet unborn, to help her be strong so that she would not place the added burden of her tears alongside his already crippling sorrow.

To lessen the dread of their parting, he bid her sleep and when she awoke, he was gone. Again, she was as before, a majestic White Raven with feathers that glowed as if kissed by a light from beyond the Stars. While she'd slept, his silent words had penetrated her soul. He'd told Raven that she should forget him, that he would understand if she found a new mate. He'd gently whispered to her that he doubted Lightning would keep her promise that they would meet again in seven years, for Lightning was flighty and not to be trusted. She was wild with power, sending her fire across the Skies each time she found displeasure with the People.

White Raven heard his words, and in this silent language all their own, she too cried out to his heart that she would wait, that she would not seek another. Never would she forget the one who gave reason for her accepting the life-sustaining air from Father Sky, and as she waited, she would use the time wisely, sharing the Wisdom of her Love. She would be his voice, guide others who wandered lost and unsure, to the path of goodness and honor. She would gaze toward the island and silently send him her thoughts and love. For Lightning had added another condition. He must guard the fire. Until the seventh day of the seventh year, he must not allow another to steal the flame from the Sycamore tree.

After a lifetime, seven years have passed. Parting from the Wind, White Raven glides to the mountain—to the very place he has told her to wait. Changing again into a woman, she scans the valley and meadows below, searching, ever searching, quickly, for time slips away. The human garments weigh heavy upon her delicate frame. Will he come? Do the fates play with their love, toss it about on the swiftness of eternity, only to tempt them again with the promise of what might be? Ah... to know him again, so close yet so far.

Time is her enemy, fleeting, even as she prays to the Spirits to slow its passing. The Raven unravels her long shiny hair, setting it free to fly about her worried face. The warmth of the Sun feeds into her newly acquired body, a warmth uncommon for this time of the year. Although it is still the Winter of the Falling Stars, Spring has sent a day from her season as a gift for the lovers.

Without turning around, she feels him standing behind her. The sudden rush of gladness and thankfulness silently pours out of her. Ravens smiles, pleased that the Spirits have surely heard her prayers and offered their blessing to this union. Weaken by these emotions, she fears she will fall to her knees, but she doesn't fall, for his hands reach out and take hold of her shoulders, turning her around to face him.

Gone in an instant are the feelings of sadness and panic of the past seven years, replaced with tears of exaltation as they gaze upon each other. Proudly she stands before him, allowing him time to gather his racing emotions as his glance covers all of her, as his hand gently reaches out to caress her tear-stained cheek.

From above, Father Sky gazes upon the lovers and halts time. This is his right and one not ordered without thought. The flames of rebirth wrap around the lovers and they forget all else save the glory of this moment. The splendor and power of this renewal wipe away the lines of separation as they touch and taste reality and again, after seven years, become one.

"I will not leave you this time." She speaks her words quietly but with a conviction that will not be denied. "When it is time, I will go with you to the island of fire. Never again will I leave your side."

"You cannot do this. Lightning will not allow it. Only if, or when, I cease to be will she ever release the spell. Only if we were to die, my love, will we ever truly know freedom."

"It would be easier to never see the Sun rise again than to be parted from you, even for seven seconds. I have always followed the path you chose for us, for you are wise and your heart is pure, but this I will not do. If I cannot be with you, I will die. Before this day is gone from us, even before I return to what I was, I shall fall from this place into the Sea. I will carry only that which we give and receive here, nothing more. Not the yearnings of the past seven years or the pain of wondering if Lightning will honor her part of the spell, only the remembrance of this day and our love."

"Then I too will walk to the edge with you, for I have died a little every hour of every day these past seven years. I feared I could not go on, could not endure another moment away from you. So often I welcomed the touch of the very flames I guarded, eager to offer my breath and bones as fuel for their heat. This I would have done were it not for the image I continued to see of you waiting for me at this place, waiting and wondering if I had failed you."

The Sun turned toward the horizon, not wanting to leave, but fearing to tarry any longer as Father Sky moved to unshackle time. The lovers stood at the edge and looked below to the Sea. They welcomed the rhythm of Order as she reached past Chaos and played upon the strings of their souls a melody of pure harmony. The man with features of the night and his lady of the dawn embraced one last time and made ready for their journey together, trusting the Spirits to find them a new home.

"Wait!" The air shuddered with the echo of Thunder. His angry roar spread over the mountain top just seconds after bolts of fire shot from the fingers of Lightning.

"This is not allowed," she screamed. "You must return to the island of fire."

The giant black Raven, speaking still as a man, replied, "No, Lightning, you are wrong this time. Death may be the only option we possess, but it is ours to decide, a decision you cannot change nor stop."

He stood fast, his arm wrapped tightly around the small woman with hair as white as the billowing clouds that gathered about the Arch of the Sky. Silent spectators filled the space between Earth and the heavens as the Morning and the Evening Star and a thousand lights from beyond the Moon gathered to listen. The Sun refused to leave. Not the least bit frightened by the demanding voice of Lightning, she waited calmly beside the Moon. For way too long Lightning and Thunder had forced their bickering upon the universe and it was time for it to end.

Lightning only laughed, sending bolts of fire across the Sky, but Thunder paused, his shattering bray held in check as he pondered the magnitude of the Ravens decision to die rather than be apart again.

"What kind of special gift do you possess that gives you the courage to seek the other side of Tomorrow?"

"Thunder, there is no special gift. It is love that guides our way."

"I love Lightning, I do, but I would not die for her."

"Then you do not truly know love."

"What must I do to find this love? I know that I speak loudly, that I crash about chasing after her, but I fear I am not as brave as you."

"You do not need to be brave. To obtain this love you need look no deeper than your own heart; even you can find this passion."

Thunder took hold of Lightning, even as she sought to run away. The Man and the Woman, the Moon and the Sun, and all the visitors of the universe waited as Thunder and Lightning argued back and forth. The battle went on for hours, but finally, Thunder spoke.

"There is no need for you to die. I have convinced Lightning that we must search for this love, and she has finally agreed. You may live, as you are now, free from the spell. Your life is yours to do with as you wish, as human beings, if you desire. Just share the secret of this love."

And so it was that the White and Black Raven left the mountain as man and woman, after promising to share the secret of their love with Thunder and Lightning. The secret contained seven paths and each path would be made known to them, one every seven years at this same place.

It is told that every seven years, if you find yourself at the edge of a certain plateau that overlooks the sea, there will appear in the Sky a wondrous sight—a magnificent White Raven. She carries in her talons a bit of parchment, and as the storm clouds gather and the heavens pull back in disgust from the continual bickering of Thunder and Lightning, the great bird drops the parchment into the air, and then is gone. This is probably just a myth, maybe not. Who knows? I have never seen a White Raven, but then...

# *The Song Of The Wren*

H<small>E DOESN'T HOLD A SIGN</small> with my name written on it, but I see him as soon as I step off the plane, and like a magnet seeking a part of me I have come here to find, my eyes lock on this man dressed in faded jeans, a white T-shirt, and an old leather bomber jacket, and I know it's Paul.

For the last four hours, as the plane bumped its way across the country and closer to this person I long to know, I've rehearsed how I will greet him, but seeing him, I stop, glued to the carpeted floor as other passengers rush around me.

We are virtual strangers, bound to each other by a delicate thread that is stronger than any emotion I have ever known. Six months ago he dialed a telephone number, one he knew by heart, but this time he dialed wrong. Instead of reaching his West Coast partner, I answered the phone. After telling him he had the wrong number—he made a silly remark about needing a keeper; I told him we all did, at times—I hung up the phone. Two minutes later, he called back. Now, as I watch him watching me, I wonder how I've managed to live my life without him.

He crosses the space between us and his voice, a voice I've heard every day for the past six months, wraps around me like a warm blanket.

"I honest to God didn't think you would come."

"I know, but I did... I'm here."

He doesn't touch me. I wait for him to pull me into his arms and kiss me with all the stored-up emotions we have shared over the telephone lines, but he just stands there, his blue eyes searching as if fitting together all the pieces of me he has only imagined over the past months. At first we teased; he said he looked something like a Paul Newman, and I laughed and said I might look like Marlo Thomas. But we know so little about each other, only bits and snippets, our dreams and fears, shared desires fueled by a long-distance passion leading to today, to now and the desire to know more.

I reach out and touch his face, my thumb gently tracing the shape of his cheek, his lower lip. But when my fingers brush across his lips, he takes hold of my hand, kisses the tip of one finger before pulling it into his mouth, gently biting into the nail.

The door closes behind us as the last passenger hurries out of the jet way and into the arms of a loved one, and this sound shatters the moment, drawing us back to the crowded airport lobby.

"Have you been waiting long?" I ask. "They said we were going to be late."

"I drove in this morning. I had a few things to do. Oh, you mean here? No, only thirty minutes or so. Did you have a pleasant flight?"

"We hit some rough weather, somewhere over Kansas, I think. It wasn't too bad." We're reaching, making small talk as we try to find our way with each other.

"Here, let me have your bag." Paul takes my carry-on and my free hand, pulling me close to his side as we head for the exit. "The baggage area is downstairs. Do you have your claim ticket?"

I do not have any other luggage, only apprehension, hidden emotional baggage that weighs me down. "I forgot to tell you I travel light," I say as we reach the bottom of the stairs. "Did the box I sent arrive?" He smiles, a silly little grin just touching the corner of his mouth, but it conveys enough sensual power to weaken my knees and I'm glad he still holds fast to my hand as we continue out the door and into the night.

"Yes, it came two days ago. I was going to open it, but you scribbled all over the top not to."

"Good. It's a surprise." The crisp autumn air bites at my face, a wake-up call confirming that I'm actually here and holding his warm hand, a physical reminder that he is real... a body to go with the voice.

Paul stops just outside the door and turns to face me. His eyes search again as if he too cannot believe I am truly standing in front of him. Shadows from the dim overhead lights dance in the mist above the sidewalk as he moves us out of the doorway.

"Are you hungry?"

"No."

"Tired?"

"No."

His questions are simple, but then, so are my answers.

"Look, maybe I screwed up. I planned for us to drive to a cabin in the woods. It belongs to a friend of mine, but it's about an hour from here. We can get a room down the street. There must be ten motels to choose from, all within walking distance."

"Do you mind the drive?"

"No, hell no, it's a piece of cake."

"Paul, I've traveled over 1500 miles today, and I think I can manage a few more. I'd rather not go to a motel room down the street."

A ragged whimper of pure joy escapes my lips as Paul gathers me into his arms. I feel the pounding of his heart keeping time with mine. His breath is warm as it caresses my ear, tickles the side of my face as we stand in the evening twilight, trembling, both needing this silent contact. Paul's kiss is light, whisper light, at first, but his touch leaves a burning path as he moves to find my waiting mouth, and all the months of wondering, of wanting to know the feel and the taste of him, disappear as his mouth closes over mine.

His hands hold my face as we explore each other and then snake deep into my hair, gripping hard. He pulls my head to his chest and holds me against him as lingering tremors rush through us.

"Geez, Holly, we better go to the car before we get arrested."

His voice is choppy, packaged in a forced laugh, and I know better than to try to speak. I inhale one last breath of him and stand erect, or at least I try to as we cross the street and head toward the car.

Paul is an excellent driver. He weaves his 4x4 in and out of traffic and onto the interstate, heading north toward a cabin nestled deep in a forest.

"Wait until you see this place. This time of the year, well, it's beyond description, just a riot of color. The forest is ablaze with reds and golds, and the wild flowers, Lord, Holly, it all but blows your mind. There's a trail that winds through the forest. It goes all the way to the top of this ridge where you can see the whole valley and the river below. There's water everywhere, really lazy this time of the year, just meandering along, waiting for the first freeze. Right beside the cabin there's a small creek that starts at the top of the canyon and empties into the best fishing stream around. It's so beautiful, and when I'm in the woods, I forget there's another world out there, all the chaos in the city. I've planned this for so long, now I can hardly wait for you to see it."

The hum of the engine soothes my nervousness, and I'm mesmerized by his soft voice, the part of him I know best. He smiles at me and turns on the radio, twisting the dial until he finds a station he likes. As the mellow sounds of Kenny G filter through the car, his voice again resonates through me like aged brandy as he continues to tell me of this wondrous place he is taking me to, a secret hideaway where we will spend the next two days. A journey we have planned for months... a beginning as fragile as the smallest wild flower that grows among the giant trees in his magical forest.

"There's this tiny bird, a winter wren, a silly little thing, chatters all the time. But its song is as delightful as an outdoor symphony. I've only heard it a few times, but when you're standing in the middle of century-old trees and hear it singing above you, well, it's goose bump-time."

Paul suddenly stops talking. His hands grip the wheel as he checks the rearview mirror, then shakes his head. "Wow, I'm usually not such a motor mouth. I can't believe how nervous I am. My God, Holly, you'd think I was a teenager on his first date, but you're so beautiful, and you're here. I still can't believe you're here, or how much I love you."

Our eyes lock in the shadowy light, and I return his smile as his words penetrate deep, and I'm almost afraid to breathe. How can we love each other so? I cannot take my eyes off him as he maneuvers around a slow car, and I search for an answer. His profile is sharp and confident, his firm mouth... curling, as if always on the verge of laughter. Before I realize what I'm doing, my fingers reach out and touch his shoulder, move to his neck, up tanned skin to the base of his ear. He bends toward me, bonding the side of his face to my open palm. Wanting more of him, my fingers edge into his blond hair, linger there a moment, then draw small circles with the tip of my fingernail about his ear. He asks me something about fishing as my hand glides over his face, delicate butterfly strokes that mimic the trembling of my hand.

"Holly? Holly, I asked you if you like to fish, and if you

don't stop doing what you're doing and start talking to me, I'm going to pull over and kill you, or something."

What am I doing? My need to touch him is so great. I should realize we're wired, wound tight. The very air around us is charged, fueled by the unknown, the long-distant turbulent passion and emotions of the past six months.

"I've never been fishing, and what would you like to talk about?" I move to my side of the car, pulling both hands into my lap.

"I don't care. You choose a topic."

Again he is smiling as I try to think of an easy subject we can talk about and broach the current political mess in Washington. Big mistake. We argue, our opinions differ so... point, counterpoint, a no-win situation. Soon I acquiesce, and we move to another subject. We talk about the environment, his children and mine, but brilliantly sidestep the issue of what we are doing, or about to do, how our relationship will affect others. By not addressing the right or the wrong of it, we silently agree not to analyze this path we have chosen to take, even though we both know we must talk about it, soon, but not now.

He reaches for my hand, and my need of him is almost unbearable. It takes years of self-discipline not to tell him to stop—anywhere, even the side of the road—just long enough for him to hold me again. But I don't. I just look at the clock on the dashboard and watch the minutes tick by. It doesn't help much so I close my eyes and try to hum along with the music. Paul still holds my hand and as he absentmindedly plays with my fingers, I relax, feeling all at once so tranquil, as if we've traveled this way all of our lives. Did Paul have any idea it would come to this when he pressed the redial button on his telephone six months ago? Would he have continued to call back that night, finally convincing me to talk to him, if he'd known we would fall in love? He's told me he can't explain why he did what he did that night, only that he felt an overwhelming need to hear my voice again. Seven times in two hours he called my number, and six times I told him he had to stop calling.

A chill races through me, even though it's warm inside the car. What if I'd refused to talk to him that seventh time? What if I'd hung up again? But I didn't hang up, and then somehow, over the next few days and amongst the rubble of my insignificant life, I found the courage to talk to him, to slowly learn of his life, to tell him of mine, to finally come here to this man today seeking to gain more of the happiness and joy born that night and nourished for months, traveling to his friend's cabin buried deep in a mystical forest to finally consummate a love that has grown so strong I am awed by its grip on me.

"Are you okay?" Paul watches me as a slight frown gathers about his eyes and mouth. "Are you having second thoughts?"

"No," I say softly. "Just wondering if speeding tickets cost a lot of money in this state." He doesn't answer; he just smiles and steps on the accelerator.

It starts to rain. Paul sets the wipers into motion, a delayed motion. I watch the buildup of rain on the windshield and try to guess when the wipers will engage and swish across the glass, wiping it dry for a single moment in time. I never guess right.

By the time Paul turns off the interstate, the wiper blades are doing double time. I can barely see, but he knows the way. After two sharp turns, we are heading north again. The 4x4 moves easily along the narrow stretch of dirt road as small rivulets begin to form along each side.

"We're just about there. The weather guy missed this one. Nobody said anything about rain, but I'm sure it's just passing through."

"I love the rain," I tell him as I watch the road narrow again. He makes a horseshoe turn, and we begin to climb.

The branches overhead form a canopy of shadows, like entering a tunnel of dancing leaves as the moon flickers among the clouds, sporadically lighting our way through the rain and darkness.

As Paul pulls to a stop, the headlights define a meadow of misty green and the solitary cabin. I laugh, instantly think of Daniel Boone, and wonder if this old log dwelling has indoor plumbing.

"Run to the porch so you don't get wet. No, go, I'll get the bags."

"I'm not going to run up there empty handed. Give me my bag, and that small one."

"You forgot to tell me you're pigheaded. Okay, here, but be careful when you step out of the car. This mud can suck your shoes off."

By the time we reach the covered porch, we are soaked to the skin. The wind slings the rain in all directions, swirls it around us as Paul fumbles for the key. Branches swipe at the roof and the abrasive sound echoes through the porch like uninvited guests as he pushes against the heavy door and pulls me inside.

Paul has not lied to me; this is a magical cabin and the forest elves have made their presence known. The room is cozy and warm from a roaring fire, and on the mantle above the massive fireplace centered in a wall of stone, a dozen candles glow brightly, sending elusive images flying about the room like nymphs on a moonlit sea.

"Well, what do you think?" His grin, controlled and smug, covers his handsome, wet face.

"Oh, Paul! And you wanted to go to a motel? Does Winnie-the-Pooh live next door? How did you accomplish this?" I wave my hand around the room. "I mean, the fire, the candles?"

"I came up here last weekend to clean up and I bribed an old hermit who lives up the way to come in tonight and light the fire and the candles. He drove a hard bargain, a six-pack and some new reading material. But I think we got the best of the deal, especially with this rain. I better get some towels. I don't want you to catch cold."

The cabin is one large room, plus the bathroom, with an open loft above the stone wall. There's a small kitchen to the right of the front door with a dining table and chairs separating it from the rest of the room. The opposite wall holds several bookcases, a writing desk, and a rocking chair, all under a large picture window. In front of the fireplace is an overstuffed sofa flanked by two club chairs resting on a large braided rug. Paul returns from the bathroom with the towels dispelling my worries about finding the outhouse. He stops by the fire, and his gaze beckons me to him.

"Come to me, Holly."

Paul stands with a towel outstretched, and I walk toward him. I feel like I'm floating, as if I'm part of a movie in slow motion, but the moment he touches me, wraps the towel around my shoulders and draws me to him, I know I am where I belong. We don't speak; we don't need to, and the towels, like our clothes, drop to the floor. In the dim candlelight, warmed by the heat of the fire and our abundance of love and need, we blend into the essence of harmony.

Later, as nerve endings pulse, still racked by the intense aftermath of our coupling, Paul pulls a wool throw off the sofa to cover us and holds me next to his heart. But we're not cold. Just as the fire settles into a bed of glowing embers as the mating of oxygen and wood burns itself out, our senses ease back, spent by the turbulence of our union. We have traveled beyond reality, traced and explored the topography, the living land of our bodies. I rest against his chest and listen to the hiss of the coals and the rhythm of his heart, fulfilled and content

Paul's hand moves over my bare skin like an autumn leaf set adrift by the wind, gently now, so different from the touch of the fervent lover of moments ago. I run the tip of my tongue over my dry lips, and he bends to my face; his tongue meets mine, takes over, and spreads moisture over my parched lips.

"Do you want something to drink?" His words flow into me, breaking the silence in this make-believe world we have created. "I'll fix us a drink."

"No, wait," I tell him. "I have a surprise for you." How quickly his face changes from concern to delight.

"A surprise, what?"

I unravel my legs from his and reach for his discarded T-shirt, pulling it over my head and my nakedness. "Just wait a minute."

Paul rolls onto his stomach and watches me pull his T-shirt down to my thighs and get to my feet. His eyes follow me as I open the box and lift out four bottles of wine and three books.

"I wondered why it was so heavy. I thought you'd packed it full of bricks."

I return to the fire, my arms holding the four bottles of French wine and three books of poetry.

"I'm impressed," he says as he inspects the labels. "My goodness, Holly, I am impressed! Where did you get these?"

"I have my sources, top secret." Actually, I'd spent weeks learning all I could about wine, but from the pleased look on Paul's face, it was well worth the effort. I'd brought Bordeaux, two bottles of Chardonnay, and an extremely old Cabernet Sauvignon, and, it seemed, an empty stomach. "I'm starving, and you promised to feed me."

Paul pulls on his jeans and leads me into the kitchen. Ten minutes later, we've filled a tray with cheese, smoked salmon, sliced apples, a box of crackers, a small container of peanut brittle, and we reclaim our spot in front of the glowing fire.

As we finish our banquet, he chooses a book and we take turns reading poetry aloud, words written ages ago, and some just last year. The cozy room and the gentle whisper of these words of life and love draw us together and create a protective tranquility that flows through the small cabin, validating our decision to meet this way, to learn of each other and finally touch.

We make love again, slowly this time, with a new sense of awareness not found within the urgency of the first time. And in the late hours of what's left of the night, after we bank the coals and climb to the loft, Paul sleeps. I lie awake, so filled with happiness yet more afraid than I have ever been in my entire life. We'd come together with such ease as if we had known and loved and touched all our lives. The storm has passed, at least outside. But as I look out the window in the loft at the dark skies, awakened now with stars come out to play after the storm, I tremble at our vulnerability.

At first, months ago, we just talked. Nothing specific. In fact, our conversations were decidedly impersonal, about any and everything. We laughed and argued, one disagreement so intense Paul threatened to hang up, saying he would never call again, shouting at me that he had better things to do than argue with an idiot. He did hang up but called back to apologize. Not because he thought he was wrong, but for calling me an idiot. That night was the first time Paul said he loved me, but it was not the last time he lost his temper and hung up on me.

Our talks started out as a safe game, a fantasy really. We soon realized we could say and feel or believe anything we wanted to. We could pour out our secret hurts and packed-away dreams, even say I love you and pretend we meant it. It was all make-believe, just a game, until three months ago when our secure little masquerade fell apart. At first, we fought. Paul would lose his temper and hang up on me if I brought up a subject he didn't want to talk about. I've always been a realist, and there were things we needed to consider, but not Paul. He would either change the subject or simply get angry and hang up. I'd be so upset I would not pick up the phone when he'd call back, letting the machine retrieve my calls. This went on for weeks until I stopped bugging him. During this time we became adept at playing other games, so well we managed to convince ourselves that we were mature, intelligent adults and could continue our dialog, trying not to fight, without having to address the constant change in our relationship. It worked, for a while, until we no longer could deny we had moved past the game, until we knew and could finally talk about the reasons we fought, that the fights were just a smoke screen to hide what we refused to accept, until now.

I watch him sleep and tuck the past away. His arm rests so naturally across my chest, binding me to him, a bond I have wished for so long.

———————

I wake to the aroma of coffee, and without opening my eyes, I reach for Paul. But he's gone. A rush of panic washes over me, forcing me fully awake. He sits by the bed, dressed, watching me as he sips from a large mug, and I inhale deeply the breath that seems stuck in my lungs.

"I thought you'd gone. How long have you been up?"

"About an hour, and where would I go without you? In fact, lady, you had about five more minutes before I was going to wake you up. It's a glorious day, so get dressed. I've got breakfast all packed. We're going to the woods."

Again, Paul does not lie. Though the air is brisk, the storm is gone, and the forest smells fresh and clean and penetrates my dormant senses left too long in the city. Paul replaces my trench coat with a Barbour jacket, adding a wool scarf, leather gloves, and a pair of hiking boots shimmed up by three pairs of socks, all too big but warm. Looking like a little kid playing dress up, I follow him into the woods as a choir of birds sings their morning song.

Gaining a rhythm in my giant boots, I'm mesmerized by the beauty around me. All the splendors of early autumn abound along the trail and my eyes are a substitute for my forgotten camera as I inhale the damp fragrance of the pine and fir trees. Even the tamarack and white cedar share a portion of their natural bouquet as the sugar maple and yellow birch vie for a share of attention, their turning leaves performing their annual dance before falling to the forest floor. The magnificent colors beckon the soul; the lush red and gold of the leaves, the brilliant wild asters, ribbons of purplish fireweed, set off by the white of Queen Anne's lace, all lie before me as if splashed from the tip of a mad-man's brush.

We stop for breakfast deep in the forest where the creek flows into the stream, using a large flat rock for our table. Paul unpacks a thermos of coffee, apples, some soft cheese, and a loaf of French bread. After breakfast, we leave the picnic basket by the side of the track and trudge through the forest and head to the top of the ridge, basking in its beauty as we tease and discover each other again.

"I think I might cry," I whisper, trying to grasp what's before me. We've reached the end of the trail and stand at what seems like the top of the world. The river below meanders through the valley like an iridescent blue ribbon adorning an evening gown of rich autumn hues. Paul stands behind me, his arms wrapped around my shoulders, his warm breath on my neck, and I know I could stay here forever. Tears fill my eyes, and not just from the beauty of this place. I tremble and push into Paul, gather strength from his presence, and promise myself I will not ruin our time together with silly tears.

Never again will I hurry time. It's so limited now, less than thirty hours before I must leave him and fly back to my empty world. Turning in his arms, I kiss him, a kiss so deep I all but forget the beauty of this place—lost in a vortex stronger than the gravity that holds us on this mountain top—lost to all reason except the power and urgency of our love.

Later, we wander the forest for hours, ending back at the stream. We challenge each other to strip and jump into the water, silently wishing we were twenty years younger, but age and reality hold fast, plus the water is too cold. We abandon our coats and boots and retrieve the basket and our lunch. And cold or not, we're soon wet from the stream as we playfully splash about its banks. The sun joins our party, and as we finish the last of the bread and cheese, washed down by wine cooled in the stream, her warmth dries our clothes and toasts our faces.

Paul has brought along the books of poetry, a mixed bag of Coleridge, Blake, and Tate Morgan. We find a bed at the foot of an ancient pine, softened by layers of needles and leaves deposited over the centuries, and read until we doze, relaxed by the wine and warmed by the sun.

Waking to the sweetest sound I have ever heard, I rise and know Paul hears it too. He motions for me to be still as he looks around us for the source of this music and an incredible smile covers his face as he points toward a fallen, decaying log. At first I see nothing, only the rich color of yellow and purple violets, the creeping leaves of shining evergreen. Then I see two little birds, no bigger than a gray-feathered minute. They are such busy tiny souls, not singing now, just flittering about the log, chattering away like an old married couple disagreeing about some silly item not worth their time. We sit so still, almost holding our breath, and listen to their squabbles, trying not to laugh and scare them away. Paul holds my hand, and I know even before he whispers in my ear that these are winter wrens, the singers of the marvelous song he'd told me about last night.

All at once, as if deciding to put aside their quarrel, they abandon their busy chattering, their marching to and fro and again, begin to sing. The melodious song takes center-stage, accompanied by a gentle breeze as it ruffles through the bright autumn leaves, plucking them loose like fingers on a harp, to float to the ground. We're enraptured as we share their wondrous sonata, and I am no longer able to hold back my tears. With as little movement as possible, I slip into Paul's open arms, and we hold each other as the beauty of this moment wraps about us, and I silently beg time to stand still.

And it does, for a while. We sit in the shady glen, listening to our exclusive concert, and I am lost to the feel of Paul, of his hands as they unconsciously caress my body. I am oblivious to life itself, wondering what I have ever done to be rewarded this way. With gentleness beyond belief, we give way to our need to make love, this time guided by the beauty and elegance of the song of the wrens.

Our warm bed among the leaves slowly begins to cool, just like the heat created by our need to feel the gentle intimacy when we touched. We collect our jackets and the basket and pull on our boots and look around for the wrens. But they're gone. We walk arm in arm back to the cabin, and even though we'd banked the fire, a cold room greets us, matching the chill that has accompanied us home after the sun left us, deciding she must go play hide-and-seek with new rain-threatening clouds.

As Paul relights the fire, I clean out the basket and start dinner, light pasta, a salad, and the bottle of Bordeaux. After I've cleaned the dinner dishes, Paul stacks the old phonograph with his favorite music and we dance in one spot for an eternity until Paul suggests a dip in the tub, which is small, but somehow we manage to soak away some of our sore muscles brought about when city folks try to be mountaineers. High in the loft, buried deep in the feather mattress, we travel the world with stories of past adventures and of the places we will go together. And as we watch a magnificent light show in the sky, staged by the moon and stars that have chased the storm clouds away, we don't make love, just ease into a peaceful sleep locked safely in an embrace.

The next morning I'm up first, kissing my loved one awake before going to the kitchen to make coffee. We dress quickly and eat breakfast. We are going fishing. It doesn't matter that I don't know how to fly-fish. Paul explains it is simple enough anyone can learn the technique, even me. Smiling my most sarcastic smile, I assure him that I can, and will, learn.

Two hours later, he changes his mind. Maybe it's the left-handed thing. He cannot understand how I've managed to survive all these years doing everything backward. I honestly don't mean to push him into the stream; it just happens. After chasing me into the meadow and tackling me from behind, we decide that learning to fly-fish is not all that important. Later we change clothes and drive to a little village about ten miles from the cabin and have hot soup for lunch at a cozy restaurant, then splurge as we share a jumbo hot fudge sundae. We invade the tourist shops, holding on to one another like newlyweds, and Paul buys me a brown silk scarf with a big fish on it, my catch of the day. The day is warm, and we drift lazily throughout the village, ending at the edge of the lake where we stop to feed the ducks and then watch the sun set before returning to the cabin. We both know we are purposely wasting time, skirting away from reality, from issues that will not go away just because we pretend they do not matter.

We repeat our soak in the tub and enjoy the bottle of Cabernet. It is our last night together, but as if saying this fact out loud will make time move faster, we just drink the aged wine and pretend otherwise.

We make love as if it's our last time, with unleashed abandon, holding nothing back, if indeed we ever have.

Though exhausted, sleep eludes us. We have to talk; we both know this but put it off, again.

My only child is grown and on his own, and I am alone. I have done well enough on my own, until now... until Paul. But he faces an entirely different picture. He's married. Separated for years but none the less married, with a fifteen-year-old daughter still at home. Six months ago I knew this; he has never lied about his family. But six months ago we were just friends, flirting, innocently playing our game, or so we thought. Even when we realized we loved each other with such an incredible intensity, we simply hid from the truth, for a while, just as we've hidden it away for the past two days.

Paul's voice softly penetrates the room. "I know why you're so quiet. I know we can't put it off any longer. Holly, I love you so much, and I don't think I can let you get on a damn plane tomorrow and fly out of my life. I'm going to get a divorce. I should have done it years ago, long before we met. I've done some checking, and I can move to the West Coast without too much trouble. I know it will be hard on Kelly, but kids fly from coast to coast all the time. I hate to do this to her; she's such a quiet kid. All her life she's been like a timid puppy, but I'll make it up to her. We'll make it up to her."

I hear his words but say nothing. What can I say? That I love him too? Of course I love him, so much I can hardly breathe as he tells me of his plans. I close my eyes and draw him into my arms and gently kiss his forehead. Such a quiet gesture, but inside I hurt, ripped apart by conflicting emotions that fight for control. All I want is Paul, to be able to see and touch him each day. Why should it bother me that this wanting will hurt his daughter? Why should I worry about the feeling of a child I don't even know? But I do. I can't dispel the selfish anger I feel because of this, but I also can't disregard or still the voice that silently screams at me about the high price we must pay for what we want. Down deep, probably without realizing it, Paul knows this too. He's just told me so; his words suggest he will move to the West Coast, but that he's already worried Kelly will suffer because of us. Is there a way to compromise? Can we find it?

"We'll work it out," I say. "Somehow, darling, we'll work through this." I try to sound positive; I only wish I could believe what I'm saying.

At first light, I slip out of bed, careful not to wake Paul. Neither one of us has slept well, but I need to think. And not here, not in this bed within reach of his hands, cuddled next to a body I have come to know by heart. I gather my clothes and move quietly downstairs. I dress quickly and leave the cabin, running as soon as I clear the porch. Into the woods, across the creek, soaking my tennis shoes as I try to outrun my tears, but they cling to my face, blinding me the farther I go. Soon I cannot run anymore, but I don't stop, just walk through the forest until I can walk no more. The sun spreads her warmth across the top of the trees, turning the lingering bits of dew into fleeting silvery mist. I look about me and realize I've stopped at the same fallen log where we found the wrens. At first I smile, even through my tears, remembering the beauty of their song. Then my heart breaks completely in two.

I fall to my knees and gently pick up the still warm bird, so small its little body barely covers the palm of my hand. My tears flow fast now as I hold the lifeless body close to my breast. What happened? Why did he die? Maybe it's not the same one who yesterday sang a song surely written by God. But I know it's him. And where was his mate, the bossy little lady who fussed and chattered about before cuddling to him and singing their duet? Is she dead too? I look about but see nothing, and then I hear her. Not far in front of me she scurries about on the log, screams out her grief, trying to understand, seeking an answer no one can give her. She watches me as I push back years of decayed leaves and dig a small hole in the earth and place him there. I straighten his ruffled feathers and then cover the grave. Bravely, she jumps off the log as if wanting to come closer but stays just beyond my reach. We watch each other, both of us silent and still, just watching. Does she understand her loss? I think so. She climbs back on the log and sings a farewell song.

Her courage gives me strength to look into my heart. She has loved and been loved, but she doesn't question what has happened to her. I think the wren knows and accepts what has happened, that she must follow her own instincts, go about her way, to sing or not, even if alone.

In just two days, Paul has given me so much. He has shared his love and, last night, his soul, all that he is, finally choosing a path while I stumble upon emotions I refused to acknowledge. Even as he spoke the words, I knew it was not the right thing for him to do, to get a divorce and come to me. His place is with his daughter. I know this, but last night that knowledge didn't lessen my desire to have him with me, even at the expense of his child.

But I can't let him do it. Right now he's blinded by the power of what we've shared these past two days. But what happens if it doesn't work out? After he leaves? What will he do if his daughter became ill or worse? Divorce, or even a separation, can tear a child apart, at any age, but Kelly is too young, much too fragile. She needs her father, a full-time father.

I look again for the tiny bird, but she's flown away. Is she already planning her new life? I am. My mind races with different ways we can make this work, ideas that include Kelly. Why should Paul move west? I can come to him. Why not?

I wipe my tears and run back toward the cabin and the man I love with every fiber of my being. Just as I clear the trees, I see him on the porch, searching frantically and calling my name.

I shout back, "Paul, I'm here. I'm coming." It will be all right. I love him so much, and as I run to his open arms, I'm uplifted and alive. I know our love is strong; it is strong enough to survive for a few more years. I've railed against time, the lack of it, wanting more, but I must learn to be patient. And I must convince Paul that I'm right. We can do this. Someway, without hurting his daughter, we can do this, even if we must put our dreams of being together aside until the time is right. Until we can return to this enchanted place and hear again the song of the wren.

# *Bits And Pieces*

W HEN I WAS A CHILD, I used to dream of four things that I just knew would make my life absolutely perfect. I wanted to fly. I wanted a large, emerald-cut diamond ring, maybe four or five carats, an autumn haze mink jacket, and a sailboat. That would do it. Oh, my... what a dreamer?

I soon learned that I was never going to fly. Birds flew, not little girls. I could not stand the thought of a wee little animal giving up his life just so a fancy lady could wear his coat, and not in a million years would I ever save enough ice cream money to buy myself a big diamond ring, so scratch that dream. But I worked hard and saved and I did get my sailboat.

I loved that boat. *'The Impatient'*, she was called, a thirty-six foot Farr-ridged sloop, tender at times, a racer for sure. Our family had so many wonderful and exciting times aboard her. We sailed out of San Diego in California, sometimes just a quiet sail in the bay, and then other days off we would go, straight for the horizon... to the open sea to play with the dolphins. There were a few times I ventured out by myself. Not often, but a few. Life was good and God was great.

# Ah, To Be At Sea

Sailing into port as the horizon welcomes
the sun, I gaze upon its setting, at the colors
that rival the changing seasons.
Pushed by the moon that rushes to
grace the sky, contentment dances about the cockpit
as I loosen the mainsail to capture
the last of the tired wind.
Muscles twitching from fighting the storm,
pent-up nerves shot full of adrenalin
after a hard-won race, none of these
are remembered as my eyes behold the
wondrous hues, the kaleidoscope from God
that dances above and around me.

# *Alone*

The winds freshen and the sea runs
high, raging, swirling against the
hull as I lower the tiny handkerchief-sized
storm jib and treble reef the mainsail.
Bits of the sun dance with the clouds, teasing,
playfully daring me to trust her as I crawl
about the rolling deck, checking lines,
securing gear ready to pull free and slide
overboard.
Slipping into the cockpit, I swallow back fear
as the wind gauge registers a force ten gale. The
sea screams like a wounded condor. Or is this
eerie sound her laughter as she plays with me and
tosses me about?
The sea spreads her fury over me, egged on
by the Devil wind. Waves break, form white-laced
pinnacles of bone-chilling spray, rearing high
against the somber sky as I watch an endless
procession of giant rolling swells march across
the sea, adorned in spindrift and marshmallow
crests.
The whitecaps grow larger and I hold fast and ponder
my fate. The sloop drops into a deep trough, down into
the depth of a haunted valley, all life shut away.

I abide in this valley and question my sanity, why I have chosen to enter this race, a venue meant only for seasoned mariners.

My answer comes with the roar of a gigantic wave, and I soar, rise out of the trough, and shoot up the slope until abruptly I'm at the top of the world, gazing at the most mind-bending vista of white peaks that stretch past forever.

As the wind screams in my ear, as I tremble at this astounding sight, then I know. Oh yes, I know.

# Catch Me If You Can

O NCE THE GALE IS OVER, I will find the true rhythm of my soul sent aloft by the rapid beating of my heart. I believe this as I remind myself that the mountain top in front of me is actually just a dark cloud, a splash of God's burnt cotton candy offered up to tempt me. And that the rocks blocking my way where the ghost of an age-old albatross sits waiting, fighting the heavy rain, calling my name, are only storm petrels leading me in the silent prayer all mariners say when running toward lee shores.

Then I see land. I turn eastward and hardened in the sheets as my eyes focus on waves that dash against rocks and islets to starboard. I head up and work offshore, checking my soggy charts against the zigzag shoreline.

The wind lashes my face, then stills, as if to say, "Ah... enough." I see the steel towers of the lighthouse and know I have won again, have outrun the Sirens, the Sea Spirits who wait to deliver me to their master to become a handmaiden in Neptune's underwater kingdom.

Not today, no. I am safe now, in sheltered waters and warmed by dry clothes and a jigger of brandy. And as I watch the storm clouds gather again, building a wall on each side of the channel, I raise my glass to the swirling gray mist, to the wind and the sea as the rains pour down.

Yes, I raise my glass in salute. "Tomorrow... tomorrow we'll meet again. Catch me if you can."

# *Who Am I?*

I SET SAIL, ALONE BUT NOT lonely, for I seek the truth, and this gives me comfort. I carefully weave in and out of the marina, into the bay, then out to sea. For I must find that place where peace allows me the freedom to search for the truth, a place far removed from all things worldly, from the corruption of man, the desecration of nature's bounty.

I find the wind and the sails fill with a force that drives me into the darkness. I don't need to set a course; no charts can direct me to where I must go. I follow the moon, a trail of stars, as my face is softly kissed by the mist of the sea. And soon I am there.

I lower the sails, ride gently upon the crest of a wave as I begin to call on the *Spirits of the Sea*. I am not cold as the night air wraps around me. No, I am warm, filled with the remembrance of where I have been as I close my eyes to see that which I have come to find, even as the currents of the universe take hold of my boat, indulgently moving it at will, just as my passion to know the truth takes hold of my soul.

What is the truth? I ask for answers, but I should be willing to give something in return. But what? Who am I? What value do I possess to offer this world gone mad? What feelings dwell deep in my heart that, if shared with another, might influence that life? What knowledge have I acquired over my lifetime to pass on, to impact others? My questions pull at me, just as the swells pull at the hull of my boat. But I must not linger. I cannot allow my mind to drift as my vessel now drifts upon the sea. I have come here for answers, and I do not have to search too far below the surface to find that which I seek.

I have found that you cannot run away from pain. Anguish and sadness stay tethered to your heart and soul, so it simply does not matter where your body might be.

It only matters that you get out of bed each day and put one foot in front of the other, baby steps if need be, but steps.

I have cried enough tears to flood this body of water on which I drift, but I have also learned that is not my job. My job is to move forward, to honor the ones who have been called to a new place, to give value to all they have given to me.

Coming here, to the middle of this silent nowhere, I watched my ship cut through the sea and I marvel at the beauty of it all. I cannot see where land mates with water or where water speaks to the sky, but it does. And life goes on; it does.

It is time to go home and as I raise my sail and pick a course, I feel a sense of peace because I not only realize, but I believe that we are not supposed to know all the answers. The burden would be too much, even if we understood it all. We must be patient; we cannot hurry time. As a child I tried, but as it was then, it is now.

As the warm spray tickles my face and my sailboat cuts through the sea, I make a vow to the *Spirits of the Sea*. To live each day with love and laughter, to give more than I take, humbled by all I have as I put away my questions until I am allowed to find the answers that are not mine to know, not yet.

# *His Plan*

A<small>S I GAZE OUT OVER</small> the sea, I feel so small in God's plan, but then I realize that this wondrous ocean is made up of millions of bits of moisture. Each particle is nothing without the whole, just as it takes all of us to make up the world, all the little parts that come together to become this thing we call life.

# *Wisdom More Brilliant Than Gold*

THE TETHER BETWEEN FACT AND fantasy helps us to realize how basic our existence really is, a delicate circle. I have been told this all my life; it is the way of the Great Spirit.

A very wise man, Crowfoot, a Blackfoot Elder, said in his dying hours that death is but a transition to the next phase in the circle, not an ending. It is only one phase in the never-ending circle of life, and as we travel from childhood to that of an adult and then on to our second childhood we call old age, we experience this transition. As we come to know and live the circle, we should feel no fear, no anxiety. We must simply live each day with honor and humility.

He also said that life is the flash of a firefly in the night. It is the breath of a buffalo in the wintertime. It is the little shadow that runs across the grass and loses itself in the sunset.

The simplicity of this wisdom is the breath of our soul, here and then beyond.

# The Lute Of Old

I HEAR THE SOFT MUSICAL RAPTURE as your words play me
Like a lute of old—the wandering minstrels into the
medieval keep, telling of hope, of love, tales brought
from afar.

# *Waters Of Grace*

S O MANY ROADS TRAVELED—MANY TEARS and memories now carefully packaged and placed away on my shelf of remembrance. Your welcome helped me sweep away the cobwebs and dust from a mind gone numb due to neglect. Now I come only to praise, to glance into the tide pool and see the reflection of love—so clear, holding so much promise—and I am cleansed by the depth of this sight, immersed in the cool waters of your grace.

# Giver Of Life

What a Joy to be the Giver of Life—
A delicate petal that calls to the Hummingbird
Come—drink from me, drink deeply—
and then go find your dreams.

# Sharing

*How many times do we stop and simply relish the wonder of sharing with someone we love?*

1. The Gift
2. My Girls
3. Hello, I'm Home

# *The Gift*

H E DIDN'T HAVE A PRESENT for his mother and time was running out. Tonight the People would give thanks to the Great Spirit as all the Clans came together in celebration.

Long Arrow flexed his knees, guiding his pony into the meadow to allow the herd to drink from the meandering stream before starting the last leg of their journey home from the high pasture.

He had no one to blame but himself. He had played and wasted precious time while others made gifts for those they loved. His sister had warned him, but like the grasshopper, he had not been wise; he had put it off until it was too late. He knew his mother would not be mad, for she loved him, but she would be hurt.

Sliding off his pony, Long Arrow bent to drink, but before his hand dipped into the cool water, his eyes locked on the glassy surface of the shallow pool and he saw the reflection of the Beauty of the Sky soaring overhead. The Eagle spread her wings, blocking out the rays of the Sun for a moment before gliding to a limb above the boy.

"Your mother has taught you better than you act, young brave. She does not deserve to be shamed because of your lack of responsibility."

Long Arrow stood quietly and listened to the wisdom of this Mighty Spirit, words carried silently on the wind that wrapped around him like the strongest rope, words he had repeated to himself all day.

"You tell me nothing I have not told myself a hundred times today, but what am I to do? It will be twilight by the time I reach our village. Time has passed for me to make her a present worthy of her value."

"Not so. For one who has eyes that rival my own, you are blind to what is before you. Look around, Long Arrow. Open your eyes and your heart. Mother Earth offers treasures beyond description, freely given to those who see with their soul."

Long Arrow stood tall, ready to confront the Mistress of the Sky, the Mother of their Clan, to dispute her words, but his breath caught in his chest and he rubbed his eyes, not believing what they beheld on the hillside above him. Slowly he turned back to the mighty bird, but she was gone, circling far above the place covered with the most beautiful flowers Long Arrow had ever seen.

"Tarry not, young friend, darkness will soon be upon you. And do not forget this day or the lesson I pray you have learned."

She then shot out of sight. Long Arrow ran to the place of beauty and gathered the flowers that sparkled like gold and silver—like all the colors of the rainbow that dresses the heavens after she has cried her cleansing tears.

Using thin pieces of vines, he wove a headpiece, a necklace, rows and rows of garlands to place at his mother's feet. He worked on until he could carry no more.

He knew his mother would be pleased. Tonight she would not be shamed by his lack of maturity, and he would prove to her she was not wrong to love him. For he had learned more this day than just the importance of a gift; he had learned how easy it is to hurt someone you love simply by being irresponsible. And as he gathered the horses together and headed toward home, he smiled and felt proud, knowing he had taken another step toward becoming a man.

# My Girls

THERE IS A SENTENCE IN a rather well-read book, something like: *It was the best of times and the worst of times.* There was a week, not too long ago that was like that for me. July is a special month. So many people I love were born in July. My two youngest sons, Brian and Darren, were born just one year and five days apart this past week, as was my daughter-in-law Peggy. My two brothers were born in the same week of July, and my dear friend was also born in July, just different years. I really enjoyed celebrating on their special day.

But then we had some bad news, news that would require us to stand fast and do battle, again, with whatever is laid before us. And it would soon be one year since we said good-bye to my son Guy.

Where do we gain our strength? How can we continue to move forward without getting knocked down in this world that runs at the speed of frenzy? But even as I type this I know the answer. From God, who never leaves us alone to travel a new road of anguish, and from the love of our family, a love that sustains us. From our friend, both new and old, even people we hardly know that reached out to dispel our sorrow with words of love and prayers.

And this evening, I experienced another kind of understanding, love offered without conditions, the purest kind. I have written before about my two girls, my little dogs, Maggie and Suzy. At night, after the dishes and such, I usually find my old chair, and after putting my legs up, a glass of Port or Brandy nearby, I read. I have also written how there are times when they want to talk, and the book is all but pushed to the floor as they jockey for that coveted shotgun spot until it seems they are all but wrapped around my neck. Another time, they are content to snuggle down under the book and Brandy and go to sleep. But tonight was different.

Tonight, I did not want to read. I sat with my legs up, just water at hand, my head back against the cushion, and my eyes closed. And although not exactly maudlin, I struggled with my emotions, praying for wisdom, for the strength to face the demons that always seem to wait beyond the bend. My beautiful little girls sat at my feet, for a moment, and then they very carefully climbed up in my lap. There was no mucking about; they were still, until ever so slowly Maggie placed her head gently against my heart and Suzy stroked my arm with her foot, not demanding that her belly be rubbed, just a light touch as if to say, "I know. We know."

If we listen to what is real, we must believe that all life is capable of communicating. As I rested there in my chair, as my two girls shared their love and understanding with me, I knew this to be true.

# *Hello, I'm Home*

HOW EASY IT IS TO wake to your touch, and somewhere between my dreams and the feel of your hands skimming across my breasts, a smile finds its place upon my lips. And I wear the lines of laughter proudly, for I am loved.

I unfurl my long arms into the air and stretch, cat scratch, and then kiss your mouth that calls me to you. I cuddle into your arms and then quiver as your tongue draws circles on my chest, like a tagger, marking his turf. You contain me when I melt, a chalice for my soul, suddenly liquid, in danger of otherwise trickling away. Our bodies bypass our minds and move on their own, knowing the way as you roll on top of me. I open to you, wet and eager, knowing that although we have no time to linger, you will never leave me wanting.

Each time we make love, we travel a new path; discover new ways to give pleasure with quiet feelings of thanksgiving. How precious each moment, but so fleeting, like a delicate blossom that clings to the branch of a tree, feeling safe, only to be whisked away by a wandering breeze... to fall and be trampled upon by uncaring souls. And this morning is no different. You pour into me, fill me with sunshine and joy, and then fall against my heart and call me witch, plead exhaustion, moan of being overworked as your words and lips nibble at my neck.

I try, but there is no way to bring you closer to my soul. I kiss that part of you I love so, just there, right below your ear, and feel the artery that beats in time to the part of you I love best, still buried deep inside me. I cradle you, massage your spine as nerve endings dance between us, knowing this is the last you will give me this morning. You moan, bite my neck, pinch my butt, but you don't tell me to stop. But I must; we must. It's time for you to find your shower and clothes.

After you leave for work, I spend the day finding my way with you in this place where you live, cleaning the breakfast dishes, doing the laundry. But I must be careful not to invade your space. I am only a guest. When I open your drawer to put away your shorts and socks, I empty it upon the bed, then refold each piece, placing them in neat uniform rows, like a child's toy soldiers, military straight, but then tear it apart and put it all back the way it was, your way. I still my urge to mingle among your books stacked on the floor against a wall. Each time I pass, my hand touches a binding. I flip open a cover and peak inside, but I must wait; I have other chores to do before you come home.

The market and deli are all that you said they were, and I fill my shopping bag with delights to surprise you and then wander the boulevard, ducking into little shops tucked between years of memories and dreams. The rain brings the wind that tickles my face. I hurry to the apartment, and as I dig the key you gave me this morning out of my jeans, I feel a sense of calm at being home. I put everything away and change my mind. You were so tired when you left this morning, and who knows what you might find today? The grand dinner I planned can wait. Tonight, simple is best: thick hearty soup and fresh baked bread, warm and waiting to ward off any dragons that might follow you home in the rain. I chop and peel, mix and knead, and then fix a cup of tea.

Without disturbing your order, I turn on some music and finally give way to my need to handle your books. I feel you among the stacks, volumes of words and thoughts gathered together, to be read and reread, old friends that give comfort when your mood demands silence. I pick a small book of Keats and my fingers caress the leather, old and worn. But it's your scent that stirs my blood. Clutching the book, I will you here, but of course you do not appear. I'm not much of a witch after all, but then maybe I should try harder, because I want you so. I want your hands and mouth touching me. I close my eyes and sip my tea and the music reminds me of the day we met, stuck in a crowded airport, waiting, hoping to hear our flight number called, impatient to resume our misplaced lives. You offered me your seat and then overpowered me with your presence, and I never shut up. How did you ever manage to listen to all my foolish talk? But you did. We were not looking, but we found each other that day and then held on tightly, finally arriving at this place in our lives.

The rain beats a cadence against the window as I watch for you. You called to tell me you were on your way, like so many other times, a moment taken from a hectic schedule to put my mind at ease. But your voice echoed my fears that these past few weeks have taken their toll, pushed you near the edge, worries about your family, and the changes at work. Have I added to this burden? Should I have waited to come here? Maybe, how can I know? I only know that when you walk through the door, I will try to give you what you need most, somehow find the wisdom to see beyond the obvious and fill your needs, not mine.

"Hello, dear, I'm home." I hear the humor in your playful words, the smile in your voice before I see your face as I close the oven door and place the hot bread on the tile and remember when you told me of wanting to chase me down and have me on this very counter. But when you wrap your arm around me from behind, your sigh tells me the truth.

I turn so easily against you, hold your face in my hands and kiss your open mouth. I kiss you, hoping you feel the storm that brews within me, a storm as strong as the one Mother Nature has unleashed outside.

"Hello, yourself," I whisper against your eyes, your neck, returning to your mouth. "My God, you're soaked. Take off your clothes and I'll get a towel." Soon you are in warm-ups and dry socks. The bread is too hot to cut, but we do it anyway, dressing it with thick pieces of butter as we dip it into the hot soup, and I cannot help myself as I lick a drop of melting butter from your mouth. We make small talk at first until we realize we don't need it, and soon we are full, stuffed like wood ticks.

The beat of the rain and the soft music lull us into a state of tranquility as we lie on the sofa and I hold you against my heart. My fingers ease away the tension of the day, softly kneading your temples as you roll your shoulders and neck, and soon you sleep, your mouth slightly open, sleep sounds entrusted into my care. You push deeper into me as you relax and give way to this primal need.

When the music stops, you wake. Mother Nature has decided the world must rest, and as the power fails, you move against me like a squirming kitten, mutter undecipherable noises before opening your eyes. "What time is it?"

"It's time to go to bed," I tell you and flex under your weight. You shift and roll to the floor like a top and scratch, as a man scratches when he wakes, and then you reach for my hand, pulling me up and into your arms. When we reach the bedroom, I feel your gaze; even in the darkness I know by the way you breathe that sleep has become secondary. Your fingers work at the buttons on my shirt, my jeans, and in seconds I stand before you draped in wisps of fleeting moonlight stealing through the storm and the overhead skylight. As your eyes hold mine, your hand glides the length of me, cupping the same spot that cried for your hand earlier today, and I whimper softly from need and desire. We fall onto the bed and the pursuit begins. I lead, and you quietly acquiesce, always the gentleman, my gentle man. I have no plan, just a need to possess all of you. I move over you with the recklessness of a moth but the determination of a butterfly whose quest it is to gather all she can. I absorb each quiver as you move under me, and I am aroused anew by the song you sing to me as my mouth gathers you in. And as any good butterfly, I do not rush my task, just slowly pull all your sweetness into me as I luxuriate in this bond we share. But when you fill me again and again, when your hands snake into my hair and you pull me to your lips, I know this butterfly has only begun to soar.

Later, much later, after it all comes together, when the air stills and we are afraid to breathe lest we lose a glow more reverent than all the mysteries of the universe, we sleep.

# *The Journey*

*So many times we rush about in such
a hurry that we miss the simple message of life and
never truly understand what gifts have been given to us.*

1. The Voice of Silence

# The Voice Of Silence

SPRING AND WINTER PLAY A game of tug-of-war in the town where I have lived for the last three years, a small town, nestled in the middle of a river valley on the edge of the Bitterroot wilderness. This quarrel is nothing new; it happens every year and is simply part of the cycle of living in the Pacific Northwest, but the sturdy Hawthorn and the Wild Plum trees have decided not to wait for this struggle to end and have blossomed anyway, covering the meadows beside the swollen river that rushes through the valley on its journey to the ocean in a blanket of brilliant pink and white.

Today I will walk into town. I have stayed cooped up, hiding from the neighbors and reality far too long. Besides, it is a beautiful day.

Although the streets are almost empty, I see a woman watching me. Over the last few months I have learned to read faces. I can tell, just by the way people stop and look, if they will turn away or come toward me. If they do come, they touch, reaching out to hold my hand or caress my arm, gently, not lingering long. It is not the touch that cut deep, just their words, well-meaning words that tear into wounds that try so hard to heal.

"You're Ms. Kennedy, aren't you? I don't want to bother you. It's just that I've been meaning to send you a card.

Actually I should have called you, but well, I just want you to know how much we've prayed for you. My nephew is Joey Brooks; well, he was one of the lucky ones. You got him out safely and our whole family is beholding, and I wanted to tell you that we hope you are feeling better, that all your burns have healed okay. What a tragedy, oh my, those two lost babies. Poor Annie and Caleb. This town's never seen such a God-awful hurt as that day. We never had such a fire. Well, I won't keep you, but you take care now, and if you need anything, anything at all, please, you just call us."

Today was going to be different. I'd even made a list of chores to do. Now, as I watch Mrs. Brooks walk away, I know I cannot continue about my business any more than I can turn away from what her well-meant words have brought back from the shadows. The awful grip of hysteria, the terror, the demons I hide from, demons that penetrate deep beyond reason or courage, beyond every effort I have pursued these past four months simply to save my sanity.

I'm so cold, and all thoughts of buying a few groceries before heading back home fly away like the fallen leaves that rise up from the gutter, gathered by a gust of wind and tossed into the sky like yesterday's trash. I need to see Dr. Owen, but today is not my day. Last week he told me how well I was doing, that I no longer needed to see him every week, but I need him now. I can't do this by myself. Why can't I forget? I want to move on; I need to find the other me, the strong one.

I pull my sweater close about my face, but it's not enough to shut out the cold. I breathe deeply, slow and controlled, like Dr. Owen has taught me to do, and soon I can open my eyes. I wipe away spent tears and walk toward Sally's Café. I will have a cup of hot tea and I will not call Dr. Owen. I will drink my tea, buy my groceries, and then walk home and pray I do not run into anyone else needing to wish me well.

The scent of fresh huckleberry pie greets me as I walk past the booths to a small table by the kitchen door. This has become my table, one next to a window overlooking the herb garden but well away from the front door where I can pretend to hide. This is where I come when I venture away from my tiny cottage three blocks away, three blocks down toward the old river bridge, one block from the school, what used to be the school, now just a burned-out shell dressed in black ash and broken dreams.

I rub my hands together as my shoulders relax and my heart slows to an even rhythm. I am safe here. Robert and his daughter Rachel have become more than my friends who see that I eat. They own Sally's Café, one of two restaurants that cater to the local folks. No one knows why Robert named his place Sally's. He'll just tell you he liked the name. He will also tell you we worry and wear too many labels. He will tell you he is simply, proudly just an American, not a Native American, although his people have lived in this valley long before the first white man touched the eastern or western shores. And even though history has lied about the Native Indian throughout time, Robert will tell you he knows what is true and what is not, and that will be the end of it.

"Drink up; it's your favorite." Robert places the blue mug in front of me. "I saw you talking to Henrietta Brooks. She means well, you know; they all do, but let it go and drink your tea."

"Can you sit a spell?"

"Of course, I'm old and can do what I want. Besides, I own the place."

"I almost lost it again. I wanted to run all the way to Dr. Owen's office, but I came here instead, which is almost like seeking his help. Oh, Robert, I'm trying so hard, and I am better. I know I am. I've worked through the worst of it. I rescued twenty-seven children from that inferno. I tried, God knows how hard I tried, but I could not find the other two. I keep telling myself I did the best I could, but even though logic tells me to think rationally, logic cannot get me past the truth. I was responsible for them—all of them—fire or no fire, and I failed."

"You set yourself mighty high, my friend. Sarah, what makes you think the outcome of that day depended on what you did or did not do? Do you think you are the only one who still carries a heavy heart? How about the school board or the maintenance people? Don't you think they wish they had done their jobs better? You take too much on yourself, but we've had this conversation before and like I told you before, I am old and have better things to do than watch someone I care about walk a road that leads to nowhere."

"You're right, everything you say is right. Too bad I can't bottle your wisdom and take a big sip every now and then, make everything bright and sunny again. I'm sorry, Robert. You don't need my sarcasm; please don't be mad at me. I'm seriously thinking of going away, just getting on a bus and going somewhere different. I love this town and all the people, but maybe it's time I go away."

"Go away or run away? There's a big difference, but if you think getting away for a while will help, you don't have to get on a bus. I know a place not far from here. Mr. Raven could fly there in no time, but it's about an hour's drive, just a small cabin up in the pines not too far from the river. I used to take Rachel there a lot before she got too old to go off with her old man. It's primitive, no indoor plumbing except cold water at the sink, just a one-room cabin built of cedar and love. Maybe it would be good for you, but give it some thought. If you decide you really need to do this, I'll drive you up there myself."

"Can we go tomorrow?"

"Sarah, I said you have to think about it. You can't jump into this without giving it some thought."

"I have thought about it. It's all I've thought about for weeks. The only thing that's kept me from leaving is I didn't know where to go, but your cabin sounds like the perfect place. Where better to rest and regroup than Nature's living room?"

I watch a fistful of emotions roll across Robert's face as he leans over the table to hear my soft-spoken words. "Well, think about this. What if you panic after I leave you alone? The cabin is safe, but it's totally isolated, from everything. There's no phone, no electricity, and even though the road's passable this time of year, it's a long way from the nearest contact, which is the forestry station and that's only manned during the fire season."

"Robert, please don't have second thoughts. I'll be fine. I need this. I need time alone, and I am not running away. Do you know that I have not cried? Oh, my eyes fill with tears all the time, but not a cry that reaches deep down to the core of me, and Robert, I think I need to cry. I need to scratch at my wounded soul, to open the hurt so that all the terror and disbelief can drain away, until the blood comes to the surface and makes it clean again so it can heal."

Of course, we did not leave the next day. Although it is supposed to be spring, Rachel decides I need some of my winter clothes and takes over the job of packing. She wants to be sure I am equipped to live in the woods, but two days later, we are finally on our way.

After leaving town, Robert drives with confidence over the rutted dirt road leading to my new home. He explains all about the cabin and we settle on a five-day stay. Robert tells me again that there is no telephone, not even a pair of resident carrier pigeons. He's determined I understand that after he gets me settled and drives home, there will be no way for me to get back to town. He assures me again that I will be safe, that I can walk the hills and meadows without fear, but I will be alone except for God's creatures that live there year round.

An hour later, Robert tells me to close my eyes as he slows to a crawl. Like a child filled with wild anticipation of a great adventure, feelings I have not felt in so long, I squeeze my eyes shut and hold my breath.

"Okay, princess, you can open your eyes now." The laughter in his voice warms my heart, and I can only sit and stare at the beauty that surrounds us. I jump out of the truck and gaze at the vivid palette of color, at the wild Iris and daffodils that hug a narrow path by the side of the cabin as a gentle breeze fills our senses with the perfume from the pine trees and lilac bushes.

"Oh, Robert!" I don't know what more to say. I just walk to him and wrap my arms around this wonderful man who holds me, understanding my moment. He hugs me until I'm ready to move away and then takes my hand and leads me up the slanting steps of the porch.

"Come take a look around and then we'll unload the truck. You'll see what I meant when I said it was small." He opens the door and then stands back to let me take it in. He was right; it is small, one room filled with pieces of mix-and-match furniture. A stone fireplace covers the far wall, and an old easy chair, dressed with a faded Indian shawl, sits next to the hearth. A daybed commands the space opposite the chair and over to the right is the kitchen, again small but big enough to hold a counter and sink, a table and chairs, and an old cook stove next to a large open-shelf cabinet that holds dishes and canned goods.

"The bathroom is out the door and up to your right. I dug a new spot last month after the snow melted so it should be okay, but I'll check it out before I leave. Let's get the stove going; it'll take the chill off. There's plenty of wood, but it might be a good idea to draw a pitcher of water before you go to bed so it's not so darn cold in the morning when you get up."

As Robert continues to explain the workings of his cabin, I draw clean, crisp air deep into my chest, and his voice plays second string to the chatter of song birds, but I have listened, albeit with one ear, and at last he is satisfied that I can manage on my own.

"Rachel packed this box with several books and her CD player, and, by the weight of it, enough batteries to play it night and day for the whole week, also CD's of everything from rock and roll to Mozart. Be sure to turn the sound up, Sarah. The bears should love it."

I follow Robert's laughter as he heads back to his truck for the last of my groceries, trying to gather together the right words to thank him for all he has done, but I don't say anything because I know he does not want my thanks; he simply wants me well, to smile again.

Finally, it's time for him to go. "For God's sake, be careful. It's safe to go for walks, just pick out some landmarks; each bend in the forest can look like the last one. I'll be back at the end of the week. Try to rest, Sarah, rest and enjoy what God gives us for free. Open your heart and feel His goodness. It's the best medicine there is."

I return to the cabin and see that Robert has put the kettle on and set a cup and tea bag next to a heavy potholder. As I pour steaming water into the cup, I remind myself that from now on, for the next few days anyway, I am on my own, no more Rachel or Robert to see that I get through the day. The days I can handle; it's the fear of the nights that makes my hand shake and I spill water on the stove. But just as the water bubbles up and is gone in a second, so too are these negative thoughts. I will rest; I will not let Robert down.

Although I feel the subtle fingertips of the afternoon chill gently moving across my skin, I look past the ready-laid logs in the fireplace and walk outside to explore the wonder of this quiet place. Sunlight shoots through the canopy of leaves above me as I move down the well-worn path toward the creek. I remember Robert's words and mark my way and realize that I'm already so aware of the sounds of this place, the birds, the meandering creek, even the gentle rustle of pine straw under my feet, and I hum a silly tune as I move on.

One should never linger long in town with its restricted

way of living. I close my eyes and draw in the feel of this place, humbled by all God has given me, beauty not found in any store. Early spring ferns kiss my ankles, feathery fronds that unfold and dance about, seeking the warmth of the sun. Soon they will grow, not dreaming to be as tall as the pines whose decay of lush vegetation has fed them over the winter, but tall enough to give refuge to this year's children of the forest who will soon play hide-and-seek in this pristine setting.

I have been out and about too long. I shiver from the dampness that comes at this time of day when the sun is about to set, and know I had better find my way back.

The cold cabin greets me, along with the image of Robert calling me a fool for not lighting the fireplace before I went wandering. But maybe I don't need a fire; I can stir up the cook stove and put on a sweater. The cabin is small, I tell myself, and if I wear more clothes and keep the cook stove going, I will not need the warmth from the fireplace, nor the open flame.

I spend most of the night awake, fully dressed and bundled under every blanket I can find, but toward dawn, I do sleep for a few hours. I tell myself it is enough as I roll out of bed and stretch, longing for a hot cup of tea. Although I've followed all Robert's directions on how to bank the fire, the cook stove is as cold as my fingers, but after a few minutes, I have a good fire going and the kettle on. I need to plan my days. As she packed and got me ready for this adventure, Rachel told me about the fun she used to have, of all the special parts of the forest I must explore. I spread my pencil-marked map on the table as I eat my breakfast. She said there was a trail that would take me to a small rise above a meadow where, if I was lucky and silent, I could watch the wild life that lives there. She said there were deer, of course, along with moose and elk. Although there were cougars, I probably would not see them, and the black bears would still be sleeping, but maybe I'd see the wolves, a new pack that had been released into the area a few years ago.

I pack a lunch and make tea for my thermos and then I'm off, properly banking the cook stove. The trail is easy to find and after cresting the ridge, I find a spot near a fallen log and settle down to wait for the local residents to appear. Soon the meadow comes alive. I have never been this close to the beginning of it all, just to sit, alone and safe, surrounded by the miracle of life and time.

Verses of wisdom read long ago flood back to me as I contemplate my insignificance. Chief Luther Standing Bear, a Lakota, said that the Indian reveled in being close to the Great Holiness and that they loved to worship. From birth to death, they revere their surroundings. Sitting here, in this simple cathedral, I truly understand what he meant.

I watch an eagle soar, searching for food, and a doe as she stands guard while her young frolic about, in and out of the trees and then back into the green meadow like young children in the park or on the playground at school.

And then I cry, silently at first, tears falling from my closed eyes, trailing down my face, and just as the spring thaw brings water from the mountain to fill the waiting creeks below, my tears gather like the melting winter snow to fall into my cupped hands that touch as if in prayer. Only God and His creatures below hear my mournful cry, and I feel His love and know that He is here with me. That God has brought me to this private place so I can finally cry or scream, to tear my garments or whatever I feel I must to do to know and believe what He and mortals have tried to tell me since the fire—that I did the best I could do. I know I have to stop hiding behind my misplaced guilt, that there are other children who need me to be strong once more, and I know I am closer to putting the past behind me than I have ever been. If only I could sleep, if only I could stop imagining what the last few moments of their short lives must have been like.

The last of my tears linger on my lashes as I look again on the meadow below, a different picture this time, so soft, like one that hides behind a piece of lace. The eagle is gone, so are the deer, and, as I wipe away the last remnants of my selfish remorse, a sense of peace washes over me and I know they have just moved on to complete their day. They need to feed their young and get ready for the night and I need to do the same, even though I am the only one who will sit at the table this night.

I have no trouble finding my way back down the mountain, but as I reach the last stretch of the forest and the path leading to my cabin, I hear a wrenching sound, like the cries of a child, but no child would be out here in the wilderness. It has to be an animal. What did Robert tell me about the animals? Well, it doesn't matter because this is defiantly a call for help and as I step out of the trees into a clearing, I see her. Not more than twenty feet away is a gray wolf caught in a trap. Her teeth attack the steel jaws that hold fast to her bleeding foot and she stops only long enough to throw back her silver head and call out in anguish, until she senses that I am there. She smells me, I think, even before she sees me and as we exchange glances, each one deciding what to do next, I think I see her acquiesce by slightly lowering her eyes for a moment, as if knowing I am her only chance to be rid of the trap. I start to run toward her, but something tells me to walk slowly and to keep my voice low, if I speak at all.

But I do speak. I tell her not to be afraid. I will try to help her, but even as I say these words, I don't know what to do. I know I need to loosen the trap, but how? Her foot is bleeding and as I drop to the ground and reach out my hand toward her foot and the trap, her eyes and a low growl tell me she is not beyond tearing me to pieces if I hurt her. Praying I am doing the right thing, I reach for the jaws of the trap and, although I try not to cause movement, she growls again, different this time, as if she has endured all the pain she can.

I need to find something to hold the trap open so I can try to pull her leg out and not have the jaws snap back and catch her again. I find a fallen pine branch and break off the small end until I cannot break it anymore. I need the thicker part to hold the jaws open. Again, something tells me to hold the branch low against my leg as I hurry back to her. Just as I reach her side, I sense we are not alone, and as I look over my shoulder, I see another wolf. I have just assumed she is a she, but I know this one is a male and never have I seen a more magnificent animal. He has stopped not far from us and stands very still, his head held high and regal, and as the last rays of the sun turn his shiny coat a silver radiance, I again wonder what to do.

I simply do what I have always done in my classroom. I try to be calm and communicate. I tell him to please understand that I need to help his friend, or his mate, and then turn back to her. Again, I slowly reach for the trap, but as I try to measure with my eyes, I know the branch is too big. I can't wedge it between the jaws without prying them open and this maneuver will cause her more pain. I look around for a rock and find one near my foot. I tell her what I am going to try to do and she looks at me, I swear, rolling her eyes, as if to say, "Lady, just get on with it." I take my scarf and place it as close to her leg as I can get it as I wedge the rock between the steel jaws. I have to turn the rock to create a wider opening, praying it will hold, and it does. I take the branch and push it next to the rock and quickly move the scarf lower until it covers her leg and gently pull her from the trap.

At first, I only know that I am crying, and then I realize that I am crying and rocking back and forth and that the wolf is sitting in my lap, deciding if she wants to lick my face or take a bite out of it, and the big male wolf is gone. We both jump when the rock and the branch fall free and the trap snaps shut not far from my leg. I can't help it; I hold her closer, for a moment anyway, until she lets me know with her low growl that enough is enough. But as she pulls free and tries to stand, we both know she is hurt too badly to walk on her own. I tell her I will carry her back to the cabin and, in the one-sided language I'm trying to use, she seems to question this plan. Again, I tell her this is what we must do so I can take care of her leg, but when I try to lift her, I can't.

She senses him first but does not growl, and as I turn to see what has brought her so alert, she pushes into my leg, demanding contact. He is a tall man, with silver hair and eyes the color of midnight. His face carries the lines of life and the sun, although Robert would say he just looks like the rest of the people who used to live here about.

"Looks like you need some help."

"Where did...? Yes, I need... I mean, yes, I need help. She's hurt and I need to get her back to my cabin, but I can't lift her, and she can't walk on her own."

"I think between the two of us we can get her there. You lead the way, and I'll carry this little gal. Grab that trap. We can't leave it here."

This time I know I have failed to bank the cook stove. The cabin is so cold I tremble as I search for a match to light the oil lamp on the kitchen table and by the fireplace.

"How long you been gone? Your fire is as dead as last year's roses. Get me a blanket to put her on and I'll get a fire going."

"I can start one in the cook stove. I thought I had it banked so I could just stir it up and get it going again."

"What you got against the fireplace? That old cook stove is not going to get this place warm, not in a million years, and she's shaking real bad. Get the blanket, and then we'll clean her leg."

I pull a blanket off the bed and then get the first aid box. "Do you think she will let us stitch up her leg?"

"No way. She'd only pull them out. Let's just get it cleaned as best as we can. We'll wrap it up with a bandage and even though she'll pull that off before morning, we have to do anyway. I want to put some of Robert's salve on it before we wrap it. It should be on the top shelf of the cupboard, in a bright-red can."

"How do you know that? Do you know Robert?"

"Sure, everyone knows Robert. He's real good at fixing things."

I find the red can and hand it to him. "My name is Sarah."

"Hello, Sarah. White folks call me Joseph. There, that should hold her for a while. I better get a fire going. It's colder than a mountain top in here. Why don't you work on the cook stove and then put the kettle on?"

I don't want to argue with him about the need for a fire, so I do as I am told. When I return with two cups of tea, a fire is full ablaze, turning the room into a warm cocoon complete with shadows that dance on the walls from the light of the flames. Joseph has wrapped the blanket about her and is feeding her some dried meat he has pulled from a pouch.

"Her mate was with her—at least I think he was her mate—a big male, but he left before you arrived."

"He probably heard me walking up the road. They can hear noise coming from miles off. He might have stayed with one human around, but not two. I best be on my way. I think she'll rest now. I put something on the meat that will help her relax and sleep. I'll try to stop back by in the morning. If she should wake up, just do like you were doing before I showed up. Looked to me like you two had already come to some sort of an agreement to get along."

"Thank you. I don't know what we would have done without your help. One more thing... I know this might seem like a strange request, but will you wait until the fire burns down and then help me put it out?"

I can tell by the way he looks at me that he thinks I am deranged, and maybe I am, but I cannot go to bed with the fire going. I just can't.

"No. I mean, yes, I can stay, but no, you can't put the fire out. First of all, why would you want to do that? And second, Sarah, I built this fire to burn all night. You might be able to bundle up, but she isn't used to covers. She needs to be warm. Look at her; she is still shivering, and not just from the shock of her accident. It's darn cold in here, and again, why would you want to put it out?"

How can I explain to him that I am afraid? He would not understand; no one really understands. "It's a long story. I don't sleep very well, but if I should fall asleep, something might happen with the fire and, well, what if she got burned? What if the cabin burned? It's not my cabin, you know. How would I ever explain to Robert if something happened to his cabin?"

Joseph just looks at me, intently, as if this is the first time he really sees me. "Well, Robert would understand. He's like that, but if you don't feel safe, then how about I stay? You can sleep and I'll watch our gal, and the fire. I've spent more than my share of nights in front of this fireplace. Believe me, nothing is going to happen, but I can see now that you need to rest."

That settled, I fix us something to eat as Joseph heats more water. He pulls another packet out of his pouch and fixes us a drink made with some special herbs, so he says. I tell him jokingly that his pouch must hold a lot of magic because I have never tasted such a soothing cup of tea.

When it is time for bed, Joseph says, "I'll take a stroll outside while you get ready for bed."

After a quick trip up the path, I hurry to find my gown and jump into bed. When he returns, he checks the cook stove—he doesn't trust me I guess—and then turns off the oil lamps. He pushes around the logs in the fireplace, placing one log deep in the back. The glow from the fire offers a soft light and the faint crackle and snap play a delightful melody. I stretch my sore legs and point my toes, bringing about a momentary cramp.

"Sarah, why don't you take a few deep breaths? I can hear your tension way over here. Luna has fallen to sleep. No wonder you're tired; you have to relax. Has no one ever taught you how to relax?"

"You don't understand. I have... Well, that's why I came up here, to learn how to sleep, and relax, I suppose. How do you know her name is Luna?"

"I've met her before. Why don't you tell me what it is I don't understand, that is, if you've a mind to? Or just tell me a bit about you. I already know you have a natural way with animals. I bet you're a teacher."

"Yes, I am a teacher, or I used to be." I ponder my last words and then take the deep breath he says I need and slowly begin to tell him my tale.

---

I awaken to the sound of birds and a gentle breeze that has come inside through the open door to tickle my face. I look around and find the room empty. Joseph is gone; so is the wolf, Luna. I cannot believe I did not hear them go, but just as I get out of bed and head toward the open door, he enters carrying her, which she doesn't seem to mind. In fact, she looks alert and at peace.

"Good morning, Sarah," he says. "We thought you might sleep all day. Why don't you pull on some shoes? I reckon you might need to use Robert's new bathroom. I'll just put Luna down and then start your breakfast."

Like walking in a dream, I do as I'm told. I laugh as I imagine the picture I make, dressed only in hiking boots and an old cotton gown and a sweater two sizes too big, with my jeans and shirt thrown over my shoulder, waltzing up the green path to the brand new outhouse, and I'm laughing. When was the last time I laughed? As I retrace my steps back to the cabin, I look for the male wolf, but he is nowhere in sight and as the smell of bacon pulls me toward the tiny kitchen, I forget him and realize I am hungry.

"Joseph, I have a question. Where did you come from? I mean, Robert told me there was no one near here."

A slight smile spreads across his face as he fills a cup with coffee. "Oh, a few of us wander around these woods all the time. We have a camp not too far from here and I just happened to be out for a stroll yesterday. I'm sure glad I chose to walk your way. If you want, I'll take you to the camp today."

I smile, and he takes this for a yes. "Okay, eat up and then we'll go. I'm going to make a bed for our gal on the front porch. She'll be better outside."

Again, I do as I'm told, and soon we are on our way. I follow in his footsteps because there is no path but I trust that he knows where he is going. In fact, Joseph, who has entered my life so suddenly, seems to know more about what I need than I do. As I trudge along behind this giant of a man, I feel so alive, so safe. I did sleep well last night, and today I move along with a light heart and a spring to my step, a feeling almost forgotten these past few months.

"Here we are."

I am so lost in my thoughts that I do not realize Joseph has stopped and I bump into him. "Sorry," I say and move to his side and gaze at the tiny camp below us. There are about six teepees grouped around a fire, each one covered in stretched hides painted with colorful scenes of some primitive hunt. The people wave and call out to Joseph.

He waves back and takes my arm as we move among his people. A few dogs raise their heads at the sound of us but decide there is nothing to be alarmed about and return to their rest. An old woman, bent with age, comes toward us. She is dressed in a colorful blouse and long skirt that reaches to the top of her beaded moccasins. A delicate necklace of shells and beads jingles with each step she takes.

"Welcome," she says, taking my hand. "We have been expecting you." Not waiting for a reply, she leads us to a blanket placed near the stone fire pit and motions for us to sit. Before I realize what is happening, we are served a lunch of beans mixed with shredded meat and herbs and some corn cakes. I watch Joseph crumble the tiny corn cakes into his bowl and he tells me to eat up.

I take up my spoon and eat, hardly aware that I am hungry, again. As I eat, my eyes and mind take in the activity around me. I have so many questions, but even before I can ask, the ancient one called Little Bird tells me that I must take my time to eat, to enjoy what has been placed before us by the One who has given us life. She raises her thin arms to the sky and quietly sings a melodic chant, a prayer of gratitude, and then she sits beside me and starts to tell me a story of their People.

"A long time ago, the Great Spirit was very troubled. He spoke to the animals first and told them that the Man from another place would come soon and those who had lived so long in peace and harmony would have to adapt or perish. He told them they might have to change, that they might not be able to eat from the meadow or drink from the river as they had done since the beginning. He asked the mighty Eagle, 'If you must change what would you want to be?' The Eagle said, 'I wish to be as I am, an Eagle.' Our Great Father asked the Elk and the Deer. He asked the Bear and the Wolf. All His creatures said the same thing. They told Him that they wanted to be as He had made them. 'Why must we change? We do no harm to others,' they said. All the creatures could see that the Great Father was sad, but it was the wolf who told Him that they would do whatever He needed them to do.

"Then the Creator said that He would only ask this of them if there was no other way, or if He needed them to do His will on Earth. And then He who has given us life spoke to the People and told them they must ready their hearts for terrible times, as the Man from far off would come and want all we had: our land, our horses, everything, even the breath of our souls. 'Why?' we ask. 'We honor you and Mother Earth. We take only a small portion of her bounty, only what we need to survive, remembering to leave plenty for those who come after us.' We did not understand, but we believed, and many of the People tried to adapt, at first. Some of those who came with the Man said they would buy our land, but we are born of the earth, the land is our Mother and we do not sell our Mother.

"When the Man came, he did not know what he wanted, so he took everything. He desecrated the land; he soiled the pure waters that flow from the high places. The Man took and destroyed until there was nothing left, and this is what the People have lived on, nothing, nothing but the love of the Great Spirit, and He has never forsaken us. We have always followed His way and we still take only a small portion from our Mother. We give thanks for His love and guidance. We try to understand why the Man wants all he sees and values nothing. We wonder if a time will ever come when the Man might ask himself, 'How much do I need? How much is enough?' We have yet to be told."

She sees my tears and holds my hand. "I know you do not understand, not now, but it is important for you to know about the People, the burden we have carried. Life comes filled with burdens, but we have to have faith and trust that we will survive. The Great Spirit wrote a story about each of us before He gave us the gift of life, but He is strong and we are not, so sometimes we need Him to send us a sign that He has not forsaken us, and that is why, our dear Sarah, you are with us today. He has sent you to us so we can show you how much He loves you and so you can again find the path He needs you to follow. In a short time, as the sun seeks the horizon to make room for the moon to light our way, we will go with you as you seek your vision. We go to the Sweat Lodge."

The sun has begun to set and I have changed into my old cotton gown, which Joseph has brought with us and given to Little Bird, mother of the Wolf Clan, to purify with sage and cedar. I tremble, not from the cold, but from what awaits me within this most sacred tradition. Joseph tells me that he will be with me, as will Little Bird, who will guide our prayers. Only the three of us will enter the Sweat Lodge. He explains that others, sometimes called soldiers, have already prepared the lodge, lining the scared fire pit with sweet grass. They have cleaned and dried the rocks for the ceremony and built a great fire over them.

"Sarah," Joseph says, "we enter this place on our hands and knees, as if we are returning to the womb, and when we are ready, we will crawl out of the lodge the same way, only this time it will be as a newborn, pure and innocent. We enter to give thanks to the Creator for balance between heaven and earth, humble and meek, grateful for the four basic elements of Air, Earth, Fire, and Water. Our People have done this since we first knew this land, and we go into the Lodge to cleanse not only our bodies, but also our spirit, our heart, and mind. I want so much for you to hear the voice of silence, but although we wish you to experience what we have known all our lives, it is for you to decide if you want to do it or not."

The sun has set and the Lodge is ready. The blaze of the heating fire is now a glowing bed of coals as the soldier uses deer antlers to carefully lift the Grandfather rocks and place them in the readied fire pit. I follow Little Bird, dropping to the ground and crawling into the Lodge. She motions for me to sit on one side of the fire pit and Joseph on the other. After placing the jugs of water inside the Lodge, our soldier lowers the skin door. Joseph has given me a small bag filled with red cedar and sage and also a piece of tobacco, all an offering to the fire.

Little Bird speaks to the Great Spirit and asks Him to bless this gathering. Her tiny fingers never quiver as she pours water over the hot rocks and the Lodge instantly fills with a heat that holds my breath for a moment in time. She sprinkles her red cedar and sage over the rocks, adding the tobacco and another ladle of water, all the time praying and chanting.

I place my gifts upon the stones and give thanks for this privilege to find my way. I cannot see well, but I know that Joseph still sits across from me, and as Little Bird chants softly, I am lulled toward a far topography, to that serene place I seek to find, led by her song as I too thank my Lord for His love and protection.

It is her voice that first tells me she is here. I wipe at my eyes, push away the vapors of heat that cover my senses like a worn, thin veil. I feel her small, pudgy fingers skate up my arm and I hear her laughter, just like she has done so many times during the year, a game we played each day before she left for home.

"Don't cry, Ms. Kennedy. Look, Caleb is here too. We came because we heard you were real sad. Say hello, Caleb, and give Ms. Kennedy a hug, but hurry because we can't stay too long."

I can see them now. Annie and Caleb sit beside me, touching me; their tiny hands hold tightly to mine as they try to comfort me. "I can't believe you're here," I tell them. "I thought I had lost you. I looked and looked, but I could not find you. They told me you died in the fire, but you're here. You're not lost."

Caleb reaches up and puts his hand on my face. "When the fire started, we were really scared, but we remembered what you taught us, to always stay calm. We could hear you calling us, but we couldn't see you, and then it got hot so we ran to the coat closet and then we got real tired so we went to sleep, and you know what? When we woke up, we were in the best place."

"Let me tell her. Caleb, let me tell her this part. You know when you're in church and you look up and see all the pretty lights coming through the picture in the windows? Well, at first, that was where we were, and then we met my grandpa and he said that he had been waiting for me. And Caleb's grandma was there too. It's the nicest place ever, but when we found out that you got hurt and then, worst of all, that you were real sad, we said we had to come here and let you know we are okay. So that's what we did, but now we have to go."

"You need to go to sleep now," Caleb says. "Annie and I have to go, but before we leave, you have to promise to be happy and then you go to sleep. Just remember forever and ever that we love you because you always loved us, and you gotta remember that you are the best teacher in the world."

———————————

I open my eyes, but I don't know where I am. The light moves above me like a kaleidoscope, out of focus, bright then dim. I call out and Joseph comes to my side and takes my hand.

"Sarah, I'm right here. Hush now, you're okay. Just rest. We will stay here tonight. Go back to sleep now."

I listen to him tell me to go to sleep. That's what the children had said, that I should sleep. I am tired; I'm so tired.

I wake and hear children playing and their laughter brings joy to my heart. I dress quickly and hurry to find them. I see Little Bird and Joseph, just as they see me. The others, the old ones, are there also, sitting around the campfire, eating and talking, but in the open field I see the children playing stickball. I don't remember seeing any children when we arrived yesterday, but now the field is full of laughing children, just kids being kids.

"Sarah, come have something to eat. We must leave soon." Joseph stands and walks toward me. "You look well. I think you slept better last night. You were so tired that we decided it was best to spend the night, but we have to go back to the cabin after you have eaten."

I know we have to go, but I do not want to leave this place. I hold tightly to Little Bird. We do not need words; her look tells me of her love and that I have completed what I came here to do.

"The children have a gift for you," she tells us. "They made these early this morning from flowers they gathered in the meadow and shells from the river. As with life, the flowers will continue their cycle; they will wither and fall back to where they came from, but the twine is like the circle of our existence. It will hold the shells in place, a small and simple token of the Great Spirit's bounty."

Both Joseph and I lean down so she can place each necklace over our heads. "Remember us, Sarah, and what you have learned here. Our Creator, Mother Earth, and all we deem holy go with you. They have re-read your story in the book of time and, as from the beginning, it still reads as it was first written."

It is not long before we reach the cabin. We have walked in silence. I long to tell Joseph of the joy I feel now that I know the children are safe and happy, but I don't think I need to. After all, he was there. He must have seen them too. I cannot wait to tell Robert. I know he will only have to look at me to know my joy. He is coming to get me tomorrow afternoon and I am ready to go home. How wonderful that sounds, to go home.

Luna hears our footsteps and runs to greet us. Her limp is almost gone and she looks well indeed. "Sarah, I have to go now," Joseph says. "I hope I can come back before you leave tomorrow, but I think Luna needs to spend another night in the cabin. Will you be all right? She will need to stay warm, so you have to build a fire. Can you do that? If not, I can stay another night."

"I've been so selfish, and you have been so kind. Yes, Joseph, I will build a fire and I will care for her tonight. I will be well. I am well. I know I should not ask, but I do hope that I will see you tomorrow. If not, if this is to be our good-bye, then go with God, my dear friend, and know that I will never forget you."

He smiles, that slight smile he wears so well, and our fingers touch for a brief moment and then he turns and walks away, not quite as tall or straight, it seems, as the day he walked into my life.

I keep my promise and build a fire and after we have eaten, I lie down beside Luna on the floor, in front of the fire, and as it warms our bones and calms our souls, we sleep.

Long before the sun is up, I decide that I will go back to the village. I still have so many questions. If I hurry, I can go and be back before Robert comes to get me. I feed Luna and put some crackers and fruit in my pocket. I leave Luna on the porch, but she will not stay there. Each time I send her back, she waits until I walk off and them follows me. I do not have the time to argue with her so I call her to me and off we go.

I know I have walked the same direction that we walked two days ago, but I cannot find the village. I turn back and try again, but no matter which way I go, the village is not there. Luna stays close to my side, looking at me, as if wondering if I know what I am doing. I go back and start over, but it is not there. There is no sign of the village, of the old people, of Little Bird or the children. My hand touches my beautiful necklace. It is real, a tangible truth that I have not imagined the village or the people who helped me to find my life.

Luna pushes into me and then starts toward the small

rise at the edge of the meadow. She stops once to look at me and then back at the ridge, at him, her mate.

I know it is her mate, but he looks different somehow, older, if that is possible. I look more closely and then fall to my knees. He leaves the ridge but stops next to Luna. He has moved slowly, as if he is so tired, and I want to jump up and go to him, but I cannot. If he wanted to, he would have come to my side. I reach for my necklace. The flowers have started to wilt, just as Little Bird said they would, just like the ones that adorn the necklace that hangs around his silver throat.

I must speak through my tears as I say, "Oh, Joseph, what have I done? What has it cost you to help me heal? My dear, dear friend, it is all so clear now. All that Little Bird told me, it all makes sense now, but how I can go away, back to a life I would not have except for your sacrifice, and never know? I don't think I can bear not knowing if you are well? If you can return to what you were before you helped me? I don't know what to do."

He nudges Luna and then comes to my side. He sits in front of me, so close, his way of forcing me to seek his thoughts, and I try. And then I know. He has given me this moment and it is enough. I reach out and touch the shells and fading flowers that rest against the silver coat he wears so proudly. I lift the necklace from his neck and place it next to mine, to rest against my heart, and then gently caress him, and he welcomes my hand for a moment before pulling away, for our time has passed.

I stand and watch them cross the meadow and climb the ridge and then disappear. Words Robert has said more than once echo through me as I walk back to the cabin. I know what is true and what is not.

Robert waits for me beside his truck. "I was just about to start honking the horn. How you doing? You look a lot better than when I last saw you. How'd it go? You ready to go home?"

My heart is beating so fast. My hands shake as I turn back toward the ridge. I want to run after them. I want to shout at Robert; I need to tell him what has happened, but how? I need to gather my words so he will not think I have lost all reason. I take a deep breath and quietly say, "Yes, Robert." As I fight to find the right words, I just say, "I am ready to go home."

We walk into the cabin to gather what we brought here days ago. As Robert cleans out the cupboard, I reach up and touch the red can that holds his magic salve. I move to the bed and pick up my gown and inhale the red cedar and sage before stuffing it into my backpack. After one last look around, we head toward the truck, but I need to do one last thing.

I leave the porch and go to the side of the cabin. The trap is still there, right where Joseph told me to leave it, and so is my scarf, covered with her blood.

Robert calls to me. I fold the scarf and put it in my pack. "I'm coming."

We drive away, down the rutted road, and I almost panic. I want to jump out and go find my friends, but I don't. I just breathe deeply, slow and controlled, just like Dr. Owen has taught me to do.

"So how did it go? Rachel told me she drew you a map of all the places she used to sneak off to years ago. If you went to any of them, I bet you have a story to tell."

It takes me a moment to find my voice. Tears start to well in my eyes, but I will not cry, not today. "Yes, Robert, I have a story to tell, and one day, when we have some time, I will." I turn once more to look behind me, but of course, they are gone. I reach out and take Robert's hand and breathe in one last breath of this magical place. "One day, my dear friend, I would like to tell you a story."

# *Saying Good-Bye*

I TRAVEL THOUSANDS OF MILES, WANDERING in my solitude, sometimes sad but never silent. Winter is near, close, hiding somewhere between autumn and a chilling breeze. This is a sorrowful place so I will not linger. I must move on; I need to reflect and then let go.

I listen to the song of the Raven, which brings me joy and rebirth.

We must be born and then reborn, many times.

This is the way of the Great Spirit.

The tales I have told here of the First People come from my overactive imagination, fueled by snippets of stories I've heard all my life. There is a Cherokee legend about fire. Thunder did live beyond the Sky Arch, and Lightning did put fire in the hollow of the sycamore tree, and although White Raven tried, it was a tiny Water Spider with black downy hair and red stripes down her back that brought fire to the people. Their tale is true, mine, just fiction.

I am at peace when I follow the ways of those who gave me life. It is their tradition and courage and their love of all the Great Spirit has loaned to us that allows me to give thanks each day, for I am so blessed. We are almost at the end of my wandering. Join me on this final journey of thanksgiving, of my memories of joy and laughter.

1. My Mom
2. To Hear The Blackbird Sing
3. Remembering

# My Mom

WE STARTED OUT AS MOTHER and daughter and ended up best friends. My mom was the most beautiful, intelligent, funny lady I have ever known. I could go on and on and it would be appropriate because she had no limits, no boundaries.

Of course along the road to my maturity, we locked horns many times, but she usually took it all in stride, telling me that one day I would understand, and I have come close. When asked if I have met my life's expectations, I would have to say no, I will never measure up to her goodness, although she thought I was perfect.

It is so easy to take a happy childhood for granted. We moan and groan when we do not get our way, for a while, and then move on because there is always something new beckoning us around the bend. But as time passes and we grow and get old, we realize that life was not so great for our parents and that their generation dealt with problems we have never had to face. Such was the case for my mom.

She was the oldest of four children and, although her parents married and divorced three times, they never got it right, so needless to say, theirs was not a happy household. Her best friends were the porters and conductor on the trains where she spent most of her first eight years traveling back and forth between her grandmother and her parents. Mother wrote in her journal that she wondered if she would ever find stability. She wrote, "I never wanted to be a princess. I just longed to have a real home and to be loved." And, for a while, her wish came true.

About this time, her grandmother married a wealthy cattleman and, after pulling a few strings to get custody of this beautiful child he adored, he moved his new family to Los Angeles. Mother's life seemed transformed from uncertainty to one that mirrored the life of the princess she had dreamed about, but she soon learned to be careful of forgetting the past because it can return so quickly.

Mother's life was hitched to that of her grandmother. I guess it is only fitting that I stop right here and tell you a bit about my great-grandmother. Her name was Blanche, and Blanche was a beauty. She was Seneca, a proud warrior woman with dark hair and eyes, and although she did not carry a tomahawk, she was tough as nails.

She lived in Nebraska, her tribe having been relocated there years before. Blanche was used to taking care of what belonged to her. She married young and had two children, a son named Guy and my grandmother—Mary was her name. But Blanche had married for all the wrong reasons and it didn't work out, and from tales told, my great-grandfather, Mr. Chance, was a rounder, passionate and handsome as sin but mean when drunk, and after he left her, Great-grandmamma had to stay on her toes. She owned a gun and was not shy about using it to prove a point or win a confrontation, and being such a beauty, men flocked to her like bees to honey. Trouble had a way of finding her.

She knew she needed to move on, get out of town, and it was not long before opportunity came knocking. My grandmother was in the hospital for a ruptured appendix and her roommate was a lady from out of town and owned a profitable business she wanted to sell.

Blanche jumped at her offer. Why not? After all, her

name was Chance. Why not take one? The business was in Sioux City, Iowa. It was a brothel. Well established, it even had living quarters; one side for the family and the other for the ladies of the night. Guy grew up and got married and moved out, as did Mary, but then she moved back home. My dear, sweet mother was born there, just steps away from all the action. Nothing like having a dozen or so makeshift aunts to care for the wee child, as this was the first time my mom's parents decided they hated each other.

A few years later, Blanche met her cattleman. Mr. Fluenguer was Swiss, and although he first arrived on the steps of Happy Haven for nothing more than a night of pleasure, he tumbled head over shoe straps for the raven-haired beauty that opened the door. Like any good fairy-tale, life changed, not only for my mom, but for the Madam of the house.

He asked great-grandmother to marry him and suggested she sell her business, smart enough to know better than to demand. She agreed. He bought her a mansion, and everyone lived happily *almost ever after*, until the terrible influenza epidemic of 1918.

Advised by his doctor to move west, Mr. Fluenguer hitched up his private railcar and moved everyone to Los Angeles, but he never really regained his strength. Mom's new grandfather died of influenza a few years later and, although he left his wife a big, new mansion and enough money to last forever, trouble came knocking on their door, in spades.

Blanche was still a beauty, but after a few years, as she grew older, her gentlemen friends grew younger. They loved her generous ways and soon all the money that was to have lasted forever was gone. "Not to worry," she told Mom. She would turn her mansion into a boarding house and happy days were here again, almost.

My dad and his family moved to California after having

buried their mother. He brought with him two married sisters and their families, two single brothers, and two young sisters. An old hound dog came along for the ride. The girls stayed with the married folks and my dad and his brothers moved into the boarding house. Mom fell in love at first sight with this tall, good-looking son of a Cherokee, and although it took Dad all of six months to decide he loved Mom, he did not express his feeling until she turned seventeen. Burt knew she had to finish school, and there was no way Blanche was ever going to allow Mom to marry him because she had designs on him herself.

One day, after Mom turned eighteen, they secretly met at the L.A. county court house and got married. She missed their wedding party because she had to take the streetcar back home and bake a birthday cake for her sister. Later that afternoon, Blanche caught Dad kissing Mom, and their tiny world exploded. She ordered him into her study and when he told her they had gotten married, she took their marriage license, wadded it into a ball, threw it at Dad, and pulled out her gun. Dad thought Mom was going to be a widow before she ever had a chance to be a bride. They had decided not to tell Blanche about the wedding until they could afford an apartment of their own, but now they were out on the street with just the clothes on their backs.

During the next few years, sadness and despair camped on their doorstep. Their first child died at the age of eleven days. The Depression was in full swing, but they were lucky. They found work, that is, if they agreed to both work for one paycheck, but they did survive as their love grew stronger and guided them through it all.

In her journal, Mom compares her life to the seasons of the year. Her childhood was her winter, her youth like summer, sometimes wonderful, and other times hot and sticky. Middle age came around like fall, a chance to stop and catch your breath and finally enjoy a peaceful moment, knowing you had earned this time to relax, to regroup, even though you knew you had to stay alert. She'd spent too many years learning that problems always lurked just around the corner.

Her spring... Well, she says it best. "I count myself so fortunate to be alive. Each day I smile and total all my blessings. Because you see, I am loved! I know this each time I hear a bird sing, each time one of the staff drops in just to say hello or to ask my opinion about something. Each day is filled with sunshine when my daughter comes and we go out. We go to lunch or shopping or just fool around; we laugh and act silly or serious, whatever we want.

"What a joy to realize that I really do understand what is going on in the world. I am ninety-two years old and I can still converse intelligently with my twenty-three-year-old great-grandson. I have survived each season of my life and I think the best is yet to come."

Although she fought tooth and nail, Mother's health simply could not keep up with her spirit. She lost her eyesight and her hearing, even as her tiny heart struggled to keep pace with her mind. Through all this, laughter and joy filled her days and she never wasted a moment. She cared deeply for others, always putting their needs ahead of her own. She held on until the end, and knowing it was the end, slipped gracefully to into a coma.

The only thing my mom ever asked of me was to be with her when it came time for her to prepare for her final journey, and one of the greatest blessings I have ever received was to be her daughter and able to honor this request.

Hospice came; staff members came and told her good-bye. They told me stories about her, about her laughter, the many times she spoke up for those who could not defend themselves. The time she forced the nursing home administrator to sit down and eat the food in the dining room so he could see that it needed to be better. Word got out and people came from all over town to kiss her once more, to tell her they loved her and say good-bye to this tiny champion of life.

It was just past midnight when I heard her call my name. I went to her bed and took her hands in mine. She looked so small, her silver hair shining like a glowing star in the dark of night. She squeezed my hands and I told her it was okay; I told her that I loved her so much and if she was ready, that it was okay, that it was time for her to go with God.

We never want to lose the ones we love. Selfishly, we give way to anger or regret because we have let time slip away without saying all the things we wanted to say, only thinking of our own sadness and not what it cost the one who suffered during their final days. I had so much more to learn from this magnificent lady, and each day I thank God for the privilege of her guidance over the time we did share.

It is now my turn to be, each and every day, the kind of person she would want me to be. If I learned one lesson from my mom, it was to not waste a moment or breath of life—to put away our self-pity and get on with the life God has given us. To be aware of what we say, lest we hurt or offend, to count our blessings and share with those who have less, or maybe, at times, even more. To laugh and love and give thanks.

My mom fought a good fight, her smile the only armor she ever wore. She never complained, simply kept her faith and finished the race, and now she dwells in the House of her Lord.

# To Hear The Blackbird Sing

AFTER THE DISBELIEF, THE SILENT hysteria and anger, there comes a time to find a quiet place and give way to the reality that the ones I love so much have moved on. This takes courage, but it is a path I had to take if I was to honor the ones I yearn for, the ones who will always live deep within all that I am.

But my journey started long ago. When I said, "I do," I just knew we would be together forever, and although my husband suffered from asthma and diabetes for all of the forty-three years we were married, he managed to live a full life until one day, he was gone. The void was devastating, but I had to be strong. His sons needed a safe harbor—like Bob Dylan wrote, *'shelter from the storm'*, a storm of emotions that seemed impossible to sort out.

One night, after my sons had returned to their homes, I sat in the dark and spread out my options regarding the chore of getting my life back on track, but like a day-old picnic, nothing looked or sounded appealing even though I knew I had to get my act in gear and move forward.

I had to find a purpose. I had to stay busy. I would write a book. Why not? But when you sit in the dark to plot out a course, you tend to miss a lot. You need some light. I found that light sometime later. I met and married a wonderful man who not only promised to love and obey, but he helped me to laugh; that is until tragedy came knocking on our door, again.

My second son, Mark, suffered renal failure due to his type one diabetes and needed dialysis three times a week. He needed me, so into a drawer went the book. Mark was born with juvenile diabetes and severe asthma like this father, and from his very beginning he was so ill, in and out of the hospital, his activities restricted at home and at school. But despite all this, he loved life and he was determined to be like other kids. And he was, for a while, but he was too young to leave us, only forty-nine, and although he fought a courageous battle, he simply could not hold on.

I thought I could not go on. I would sit in the dark and tremble, refusing to play life's game. But you do go on. It's not easy, but you do. For a long time I did not want to think, about anything, especially the book, but my ray of sunshine, my husband, would not let me linger in that bitter place very long.

I turned to writing, just not the book I had put away. Soon my desk was covered with bits of paper, a gathering of scribbled thoughts and remembrances that eventually became my constant companions, the whispers of time, but it seemed like Lady Tragedy had my zip code on speed dial.

A few years ago, my second husband, a man never sick a day in his life, died very suddenly. Although I tried, I could not stay in my home. I could not out run nor hide from the memories dressed in anguish and sadness. I moved. I needed to find new space, start a new journey, but I guess I was not paid up completely.

Last year, my oldest son, just fifty-six, lost his battle with a rare type of cancer. Unlike Mark, Guy had never been ill, never. Guy also fought until the very end. He was a gentle, caring man. Even as a child he carried the torch for those in need. Guy continued to think of others and not his own pain and suffering, agreeing to donate living tissue for a research project his oncologist was conducting just days before his final journey. He knew it would not help him, but it might help others. That was Guy, the White Knight, a man who lived his life with honor and dignity. I was so blessed to have been able to spend that time with him, first in California and then here in my home in Arizona, blessed but torn into tiny pieces each day as I watched him suffer. He was so brave, so uncomplaining to the very end.

And again I sought my old friend the darkness. Unable to sleep, I sat in this silent space, lost and trembling, but this time also wrapped in a mantle of humility, for I realized how blessed I was, blessed with four sons and the knowledge that my relationship with my sons goes way beyond incredible. I would replay the years of laughter and tears, of silly times and serious times, of praying I would always find the right words of encouragement when their road toward adulthood got too rough. So many times during our travels we stumbled but held on tight and continued to take one day at a time. During Guy's and Mark's illness, these terrible times, we held on tighter, we fought the battles, all of us praying each day to God for His grace and strength to guide us. I have often thought of that moment, just my sons and me, when separation occurred, when they left my body and breathed without me and became what God had ordained, and I felt so humbled by this profound experience.

My sons were a lot like my dad, and when they got together, I am sure they drove my mom crazy—all these young kids and one ornery old grandpa.

My dad was Cherokee and every now and then he would share a tale or two he'd heard growing up. His favorite was about the Raven, and the story goes that an elder from the past could take the form of a Raven so they could always be near someone they loved... to protect and guard them against harm. The boys would listen to these stories and smile, but I knew my dad believed this tale, that the Raven who sat outside his door was really his grandmother, the matriarch of the family, the keeper of days, both from the past and the future.

We laughed about this a lot. No matter where he was, at his house or mine, he would say, "Did you see her? Did you see the beautiful Blackbird?"

"Yes, Daddy," I'd say, partly to keep the laughter going, but also because I knew, all the laughter aside, that he believed this and I honored his belief.

My father became very ill, and after leaving the hospital, had to go to a nursing home. I would visit him several times a day and he would spend a short part of each visit telling me stories. He told me all he thought I should know of his life growing up, about his mother and grandmother, of the Cherokee, stories I had wanted to hear all my life, sad stories he felt were better left untold, until now.

The day before my father died, he wanted to go outside, and as we sat in the garden and watched the sun go down, he said he had one last tale to tell. As the sun set and the chill from the beginning of night surrounded us, he told me it was almost time, time for him to hear the Blackbird sing.

Each culture has its folklore and there is more to be found in these stories than simple tales passed down from one generation to another. My father spoke of the ways of the Cherokee, and although they suffered greatly, they always found a way to move forward, taking only what was good and leaving the negative along the road they traveled.

He believed—I believe—that when it is time to cross over, the serene song of the Blackbird gathers together the spirits from the past. They come with compassion and understanding to walk beside our loved ones, to give comfort and dispel any fears that might lurk about, lighting the path that must be traveled with a radiance so pure that only joy and peace are allowed to join the procession.

The greatest gift I have ever been given was simply the privilege of being a mom to my children. I will miss my sons more than I can say, but I know they are at peace because I believe Guy and Mark heard the Blackbird sing. I believe they were not alone, that the spirits found their way to their side, their dad, their grandparents, and maybe even the ancient ones of the Cherokee. I believe these travelers surrounded them with a gathering of love and all that is good to walk with my sons on their final journey, and it is through this belief that I find the courage to smile—and to say good-bye—as I remember, as I will always remember.

# Remembering

I gently brush away a tear
And my thoughts return to when
We shared a laugh, a special bond
and all that's ever been
All my life I've loved them so
even as they loved me
And know that as it always was
forever it shall be

*bjd*

Made in the USA
Charleston, SC
16 May 2014